Extinction Effect:
Undead Uprising

By Robert Wright Jr

Dedication

For the fighters hoping for peace.

Also By Robert Wright Jr.

Table of Contents

Acknowledgements

Thanks to two of my favorite people – your unwavering support keeps me writing and creating.

Chapter 1

On October 31st, 2017 at 1:00 pm PT there were 7.6 billion people living on Earth. At 1:01 pm PT in a blinding flash, nine-tenths of them died. Or so we thought.

At that point in time, a small hot red ball appeared over every major city on our planet and exploded. Each weapon was genetically manufactured to kill all of Earth's human life forms without totally destroying our infrastructures–someone's science was a tad off.

I was taught in school that we were slowly killing our planet and ourselves. Climate change was making war on us as a species. Humans went out of their way to massacre their fellow man over differences in the color of skin, religion, and politics. We were supposed to be the generation that saved the planet and humanity for ourselves and our children. Unfortunately, we were never given the chance.

Envious eyes looked upon us from our nearest neighbor, Alpha Centauri. Eyes that had decided we weren't killing ourselves off fast enough. Not that a lot of humans would have agreed with that thought. Eyes that had taken matters into their own hands on the day they tried to kill humanity.

Chapter 2

Heoheska Light Scout 1 – Seattle, Washington – October 31st, 2017 1800 PT:

Vlury moved through the city, the light breeze blowing the stink of corruption from the dead across his nose and causing his whiskers to twitch in agitation. This was all wrong. They had been briefed about what they would find on this planet before being transferred here. So far, the situation was entirely different than what he had been led to believe. Another intelligence screw up. His whiskers and pointed ears twitched in amusement at that thought. It was true of any army, the front-line troops always felt let down by military intelligence.

Small piles of ash. That was all that was supposed to be left of the human creatures, at least in the major cities. Of course, the further you got from the center of the blasts there could be some bodies, his commanders had lectured, but not here, not like this. As usual, the briefings didn't match reality.

There were a large number of ash piles all over the sidewalks and roads as they had been told. Yet as he passed human vehicles and buildings, the scout could see the remains of even more bodies. More bodies than there should be.

Stopping at the closest vehicle, he peered at the two bodies inside and shook his head at the sight. Their clothes hung in tatters as did layers of skin that had been peeled back by the blast. In some places, he could see where the blast had taken the skin off down to the bone. They were so torn up, he couldn't even tell if the humans had been male or female despite his close examination.

The cat-like warrior shook his head at the sight, it wasn't his problem that the bombs hadn't worked as they should. All he needed to worry about was scouting his section of the city so that his unit could secure it, set their homing beacon, and the rest of the battalion heavies would be able to follow them to this planet.

The system that had sent his unit through space was fine for personnel and light weapons. The heavier war machines needed beacons to pinpoint landing spots. As it was his unit had lost five percent of the personnel sent over here. An acceptable loss his commander had told everyone. Acceptable to all except the warriors that were left floating in space or sent into the center of the planet or wherever else they had ended up. He shuddered at the thought. Being killed in battle was one thing. A noble end for a warrior, but to die like some of his companions due to some REMF mishandling the transfer was an entirely different thing altogether.

Vlury hefted his weapon and moved down the sidewalk trying not to kick up the ashes spread all over when a sound caused him to stop again. He cocked his head, listening for the noise as his eyes scanned the area for any danger. After a few seconds of searching, he grunted and shook his head. "Vlury, you're acting like a female Heoheska carrying a litter of kittens."

The warrior scanned the area again, his dark green eyes gathering what little light reflected off the buildings surrounding him and trying to pierce the darkening shadows. Reaching up he tapped the side of the helmet where his communication unit resided and growled, "This is Vlury, I am almost there." The comm gear carried his irritation and unease back to the base.

Only low static came back until the rough voice of his unit commander, Klamm, came over his communication unit after a few seconds. "Vlury, stop acting like an arrgant and move out. You were supposed to be at the target by now."

Vlury nostrils flared at the Heoheska insult. His hand unconsciously moved down toward his armored crotch after being compared to the tiny vermin that infected the nether regions of all on his planet. He scratched quickly and scowled. Looking around, he tapped his communication unit again. "There is something wrong. I can't put a claw on it, but something is not right, Klamm. There are bodies everywhere."

Klamm stood at his unit's landing point watching the last of his personnel materialize. Assigned to the city's waterfront area, they were supposed to secure it for the follow up forces and to place the all-important homing beacons. Forgetting temporarily about Vlury, he grunted with some satisfaction when he saw his heavy weapons section flicker and shimmer in a wave of light before fully coming across the vastness of space. He took a quick breath of relief. He had lost only five percent or so of his unit to the quirks in the technology that allowed them to arrive here. An acceptable loss in wartime, he thought.

His planet had developed a way to bend space and time so that the Heoheska could move objects or people instantly from one place to another. Unfortunately, for anything bigger than the bombs that took out this world's cities or warriors and their equipment, homing beacons were needed. That's where his command and units like his came into play. They were sent out after the bombs did their work to clean up any survivors outside the cities and to set the homing beacons.

He knew that most likely he would never need the heavy stuff. Most, if not all, the people in this city and surrounding areas should be dead after the barrage his own people had laid on this world. But, as the commander on site, it was always better to be safe. There would be a few survivors left alive outside the city. After all, the bomb's effectiveness only reached so far from the blast center. His unit was here to mop up the last of the humans on this new world of theirs. The mission was dangerous, that was why units like his took such hits on personnel.

A voice over the main communication unit brought his attention back to the problem at hand. "What was that, Vlury? I say repeat that last."

Vlury shook his head at the irritation in the commander's voice. "Probably wants to get back to diddling some female," the warrior whispered to the silent night breeze. A quick smile showed the two lower fangs of his wide mouth. Stabbing the communications unit button once more he growled, "I said that there is something strange about the area, but I can't figure out what the problem is. Someone screwed up. There are bodies all over the place where there shouldn't be." The wind gusted through the dead street for a second and brought back the smell of decay, causing an involuntary shudder.

The commander's voice once more fought over the static. It's louder than before leaving no doubt what he thought about Vlury's concerns. "Listen, scout, your job is not to think. Thinking is the science department's job. If they screwed up then they will be dealt with. Dead is dead, it doesn't matter if the bodies were turned to ash or not. Understand? Your job is to be my eyes before we move out. If you are not at your target point in half an hour you will not live to see the morning sunrise on this planet. Do I make myself clear, scout?"

An irritated growl escapes Vlury's lips as his narrowed eyes survey the now silent city. Responding to the years of military training ground into him he stiffened to attention and punched his communication button barking out his answer, "Yes, Commander, I understand and obey."

"Good, good. You're probably still feeling the transfer effects. Now, get a move on and we will meet you at the target point in two hours," Klamm said his voice now lower pitched hoping to soothe his scout. Vlury was one of the best of his unit's warriors and there was no reason to piss him off at the start of what could be a long mission. After all, scouts were picked not only for their bravery and daring but for their intelligence too, Klamm reflected as he threw the communication unit's mike back to the officer in charge. He marched off to talk to the platoon leader that had just arrived thinking how easy and light his losses had been so far.

Vlury glanced back the way he had come, fingering the trigger of his weapon, a slight snarl curling his lips. Taking one more glance around the buildings surrounding him, the eerie quiet slamming against his mind, he started to slither around a long vehicle that he knew the humans called a bus. Reaching the open doors of the vehicle, he stopped once more his ears cocked. There it was again that sound. A low mewing sound coming from the interior of the bus. "What the hell," he whispered to the dead around him. No one answered back. Yet.

He moved up the steps of the vehicle with a caution earned over many years of training and warfare and looked down the rows of empty seats. It finally hit him what had been bothering him ever since he had been exploring the dead city. It was the feeling of being watched. As though a thousand eyes were on him. Waiting for him to get deeper within the city before coming out. He ducked down the steps and took another quick peek around the dead city streets before going back inside the bus.

All at once, all over the world minds that once processed images of love, hate, families, and god now woke up with one overwhelming feeling – hunger. An insatiable hunger that filled what was left of their brains and produced low moans of pain and want that whispered from mostly destroyed throats.

The bodies move slowly at first. Damaged muscles and bones sluggishly responding to the signals being fed from newly undead minds. This new hunger overrode all other signals, all other problems that the bodies have. They all shuffle, walk, and crawl toward one goal. Food. The smell of live flesh, pumping hot blood, and the beating of hearts causes the undead to rise and move toward their first meal. Toward satisfying their want for the taste of flesh and blood.

"Hello. Is anyone here?" Vlury's voice bounced off the empty metal walls of the bus. Lost in thought as he scanned the depths of the vehicle, he felt a tug at his boots. Looking down, he spied two tiny bloodless hands reaching from under a seat and latching on to one of his loose bootstraps.

Pulling his leg away from the seat, he pulled at the body that was attached to the hands as they kept a tight grasp on his footwear.

With a grunt of disgust, he gave his foot a violent shake that sent the tiny body bouncing down the aisle before coming to rest about five feet away. His disgust turned to wonder then horror as the small figure turned and started to crawl back toward him.

Standing there, stunned, he couldn't help but look into the dead, sunken milk-white eyes of the small creature. The warrior was frozen in place until those small hands once more reached out and grasped his boot while the creature's mouth started to gnaw on the tough material.

The small body, like those in the vehicle he checked out earlier, was in tatters – muscle and bone showing that brought a quick surge of bile up his throat. With a grunt, the look of disgust returned to his face as his other foot came down on the skull of the creature crushing it like a fragile eggshell.

With a quick kick, he sent the tiny body down the aisle once more where, this time, it lay still. Turning and taking a step back toward the bus steps, Vlury stopped and his face went pale at the sight that met his eyes.

The bodies that the scout thought had been dead were now climbing onto the bus. Vlury froze for a second in shock as a low moan filled the air. The sound broke the scout out of his trance and he lowered the barrel of his weapon and started to rapidly pull the trigger.

Vlury watched as the slugs from his weapon tore through the bodies of the already dead. The bodies jerked and twitched from the impact. Body parts were torn from the undead, but they kept moving forward relentlessly. The moaning growing louder as they closed on the scout.

Vlury stepped back each time he pulled the trigger until his legs hit the back seat of the bus. The scout pulled the trigger and the click of an empty chamber sounded extra loud over the undead moans. The bodies of the dead Earthers reached the scout and he went down under their weight. His body armor protected Vlury for a few minutes as the bodies swarmed him, but soon teeth and fingers found soft exposed skin. The dead began to feed. His last thought was that his commander had been wrong – dead wasn't dead on this world. Then he had no thoughts at all.

Klamm's head snapped up from the map that he was reviewing with his three sub-commanders. The unmistakable sound of a Heoheska weapon discharging echoed off the walls of the buildings around his unit. "What the hell was that? Who fired?" the commander demanded turning to the head of his communications unit.

Once more shots bounced off the surrounding buildings followed by a long echoing scream suddenly cut short. Every warrior stopped in his tracks and looked up at the adjacent buildings and then back at the command center.

Klamm stomped over to the communication unit and grabbed the officer by his combat vest. Throwing him out of his way, he grabbed the mike attached to his communication set and pressed the button. "Vlury? Vlury, was that you shooting? Vlury answer me . . ." A weird low moan filled the air stopping the commander in the middle of his rant. Looking up, the mike dropped from his nerveless fingers.

Undead human bodies filled each street shuffling along. All moving in one direction. Right toward the center of the square where the commander's men were stationed. Klamm stood in shock until the wave of creatures reached his foremost unit and they went down in screaming agony. All hell broke loose then as his men were roused from their fright and started to fire into the crowd of creatures and the warriors in front of them alike.

As the undead tore into the first of the alien soldiers, their comrades lost their nerve. They saw their friends being eaten alive by the mass of bodies that overwhelmed them. Some turned and ran. For most, they didn't make it very far before they too fell under the crush of the insatiable creatures. The sound of shots and screams could be heard echoing off the walls of the surrounding buildings. As night truly fell in this part of the world, the shooting became sporadic, as the moon rose that low moan once more ruled the dead landscape.

The three Heoheska slowly tread water under the dock of the city listening to the last sounds of their comrades being torn apart by the horde of creatures that had suddenly appeared from the center of what was supposed to be a dead city.

Suzu, the unit's medic, moved closer to the two warriors in the water with her. There was enough light seeping under the wood and through the cracks over their heads that she could make out the others. "What the hell are those things and what do we d . . ."

Her voice sounded overly loud in the quiet that had now fallen in the night. A large hand clamped down over her mouth cutting off her question. Her eyes went wide as she felt the combat knife prick her throat and the harsh whisper that sounded in her ear, "If you want to live, healer, I would suggest that you keep your voice to a whisper. Or better yet, do not talk at all. Understand?"

Suzu nodded at Keiko, her squad leader, and released her breath as the combat knife was removed from her neck. It was her squad leader that had saved their lives by commanding them to go into the water and under the dock. Nasreer, the other warrior in the water, grunted softly but was otherwise silent.

A weird low moaning sound started up from the creatures above them, along with the sound of crunching and snapping of bones that echoed off the dark water lapping at the three under the dock. After a few minutes, even that sound died and the sound of shuffling feet could be heard as the horde above them moved around probably looking for something else to feast upon. As they tread water, the three watched as droplets of Heoheska blood dripped through the cracks in the wooden dock and fell into the water around them.

Alpha Centauri – Battle Headquarters for Earth Invasion– October 31st, 2017 – 2010 PT Earth Time

Supreme Commander Wavrad looked down at the small hologram globe of the planet Earth as it slowly revolved in the middle of the battle table, his forehead wrinkled in concern. He watched as the green lights all over the planet went red then were extinguished, one by one. The leading commander of the Earth invasion force stared in disgust and shame, it looked like the first of his forces were being wiped out by the Earth creatures who should have been killed outright by his first devastating weapons. At least that was the garbled, panicky information that had been transmitted over the long distance between the planets.

Wavrad turned from the image in front of him and sought out his force's intelligence officer. Spotting him bent over the communication console, he marched over trailing the small entourage that any military leader gathered around him no matter the planet he called home.

Commander Viems looked up from the communication console just as Wavrad arrived. Throwing the set of headphones to one of the communication techs, he gave a quick salute then reported before his leader could say a word. "Sir, yes, I see that we are losing all our point forces. Yes, we know that the bio-weapons did go off. Somehow, from the little information that we have gathered so far, the humans in the cities that we hit weren't killed, but have been turned into semi-dead creatures that feast on the living."

"So, the reports are true," he whispered glaring down at the floor, deep in thought. He couldn't send in his heavier forces yet. First, his point forces needed to set up the special transmitters that were used to transfer his heavy equipment and troops to Earth. Second, there was no reason to send more troops that would just be food for these undead Earth creatures. Glancing around at the other staff officers, he could see that all were at a loss. His eyes fell once more on his intelligence officer. "What is it, Viems? I can see that you have an idea stewing in that brain of yours. Spit it out."

The officer looked at his leader and then walked over to the hologram of Earth stopping before it and pulling a small computer out of his uniform jacket. The supreme commander watched as the officer punched numbers into the computer and fumed at having to wait for an answer to his question.

With a final click, Viems watched the screen until the computer beeped. Quickly glancing at the hologram then back to the computer, he looked up at his commander a frown crossing his face before he said, "We can realign our transfer conduits so that our troops land outside the cities that we hit. In this way, we can send more scout units to set up the homing beacons that the heavy units need to transfer to Earth. Then our heavy troops can transfer in and move into the cities and wipe out these creatures."

Wavrad smiled, someone on his staff could think on his feet. One of the others, wearing the red uniform of the science branch, stepped up shaking his head and wiping the smile off the supreme commander's face. 'I'm sorry, sir, but what Viems said cannot be done soon enough to matter to our troops that are on Earth right now."

"They are lost already," Viems snapped back at the science officer.

The commander looked between the two officers noticing that his staff was dividing into two distinct sections. The pure military officers in one group, while the officers from the science and communications sections gathered in the other. "Alright, just how long will it take to do this realignment?"

The science group put their heads together whispering and trying the commander's patience even further. After a few minutes, the commander was just about to lose his temper when the group of officers broke their little huddle and the officer that had spoken up before gave him the answer to his question, "One year, sir."

"WHAT!" the commander yelled slamming his fist into the officer's face. The force of the blow sent him flying into the wall where his body cracked and slid down the wall, dead.

Viems came to attention and stepped up to his commander's side. He stepped back as the commander spun toward him. Looking down at the broken officer on the ground, he barked, "Sir, as much as I wish we could change it, he was right. It will take a year to realign the transfer conduits. May I suggest that before we do that that we send reinforcements to Earth to . . ."

The commander held his temper while shaking his head at his intelligence officer. "Didn't you just say that those forces were lost?"

"Well, yes, Supreme Commander, but . . ."

"No, we can't afford to lose any more troops. The ones that are on Earth will just have to fend for themselves. That is if any of them still live."

The officers were quiet at the commander's announcement the only sound now was the noise coming from the communication area. Desperate radio calls from those still alive and stranded on Earth. The commander turned and stalked out of the room leaving stunned silence behind him.

"Viems, he can't do this. . ." his second in command started to say but shut his mouth with a loud snap as the intelligence officer turned to him and growled.

Viems took a deep breath then straightened his uniform looking around at the others. He snapped, "You heard the commander. Start the realignment process now. Anyone on Earth is now dead." The others stood still for one fleeting second then all the officers moved to their posts to carry out his orders. Viems shook his head then looked down at the body of the science officer that was still on the ground. He snapped his fingers at two guards and pointed at the body. "Get this trash out of here." Both guards moved over to remove the body knowing that it probably wouldn't be the last body they carried out of this room.

Chapter 3

Thirteen months later and one hundred miles north of Seattle . . .

Stopping under a tree, I heard a small rustle in the leaves above my head. Holding my breath, I tried to blend into the trunk. I peered above me to see what had made the noise. The dense cluster of yellow and orange fall leaves hung quietly and limply off the branches while the thick bark I was leaning against rubbed through the light shirt I was wearing.

Nothing moved in the tree or in the surrounding woods for that matter. The late afternoon sun filtered down through the foliage on this unusually hot fall day. I eased my crossbow into a better position in case I needed to get a snapshot off at anything that might come hurtling down at me from above. I stared at the leaves waiting for a few seconds, but nothing happened. I let out a quick breath and relaxed when a large furry grey head peeked out from the leaves just above and behind me.

The slight noise it made caused me to spin around, my bottom hitting the damp ground as my finger started to jerk back on the trigger. My finger paused at the small tinkle of laughter ringing in my head. "Damn, Bo Jangles, why do have to do that to me every time we go outside?" I swore as I moved my finger off the trigger and sprawled on the ground while my heart beat against my ribs feeling like it would explode at any second.

Once more I heard that tinkle of laughter sounding like tiny Christmas bells on a cold winter morning. *"Sorry, Tanya, I was just trying to keep you on your toes."* The voice echoed in my head as the large grey-striped cat slipped out of the leaves and landed between my legs. *"Besides, there isn't any prey around for miles and I was bored and you were under 'my' tree so . . ."*

Exhaling noisily, she stopped talking and I raised my head to look at my hunting partner and best friend. She looked back with large intelligent yellow eyes set above her perky black nose and the mouth that carried a set of razor-sharp teeth with two long upper canines that hung halfway down her face. The sixty pound feline took a sniff at the air then wrinkled her nose and backed up looking down at my pants.

Peeking down at where she was looking, my face flushed red in embarrassment. "Damn you, Bo Jangles, you scared me so bad I peed myself."

Hearing that jingle of laughter again I reached over and picked up a small nearby twig and half-heartedly tossed it in her general direction. Of course, I wouldn't have hit her but it did stop the laughter ringing in my head. I mean that damn pest is huge for a cat, but she sure is quick when she wants to be. She leaped into the tree and turned, her head sticking out of the leaf cover and blew a raspberry at me. Reaching for another branch close at hand, I heard her laughter once more as her head disappeared.

Lying back down on the ground, I tossed the branch over at the base of the tree. Closing my eyes, I soaked up the lazy rays of the warm sun filtering down to my face. After the last cold front that had moved through the Bellingham area, it was nice to feel the heat of the day soaking into my body even if the ground did hold some of the dampness from the recent rash of bad weather we had had.

The warm breeze that swept under the trees felt so good after being cooped up for the last two weeks. Not that rain was so unusual for this part of Washington, but ever since 'The Day' everything seemed to have been radically changed. This last storm had produced one hell of a lightning and thunderstorm. Bo Jangles' fur was standing up on end most of the time it had rumbled through the area.

Thinking about the weather we had had I drifted back over the last year and how much my own life had changed. After the bombs went off over the big cities, my daddy had predicted that the fallout would kill most of those left alive on earth. He was right, of course, to a certain extent.

The fallout killed ninety percent of the people left in the world. Which, after the bombs had gone off, hadn't been all that many anyway. They died quickly for the most part and then just dried up and turned to dust. My dad said that it was probably some virus manufactured by the aliens to work on human genetics so that when they came down here they wouldn't have so much clean up to do.

What the aliens didn't count on was that whatever was in the fallout would mutate those that survived. Some mutations were little things, like one of mine, the ability to understand animals. Some others were bigger, almost magical, like my other ability to control fire. Then there were the mutations to animals. The virus may have been geared toward humans, but it had an effect on most animals. Something I'm sure the aliens hadn't counted on. Or who knows maybe they just didn't care what happened on this world when they set off their bombs.

The worst kind of mutations, whether to humans or animals were the ones that kept you locked indoors at night if you wanted to live to see the next morning. The mutations that changed humans and animals into things that people only told about in really old fairy tales. I guess you could say that old magic had returned to Earth and not in a good way either. Whether it was a virus or magic coming back into the world, the mutations didn't happen over generations. They happened overnight turning the Earth upside down. We were living in a very different world.

Then there were the living dead. The real honest-to-goodness zombies that moved up and out from the cites as their food supply dwindled down to nothing. They moved slowly, which also made them easy to kill so that it was about three months before we started to see signs of them. The problem was that they, for the most part, moved in packs of ten to twenty bodies which could make them dangerous if you were caught out on your own and taken by surprise. Then there were the aliens to deal with. They had been starting to show up again about a week ago outside the bigger cities. Or I should say what was left of the cities and had been patrolling outward looking for any stray humans while they tried to kill the undead and the living alike.

All these thoughts were poking through my brain when the breeze shifted and a putrid scent popped my eyes open. Speaking of zombies . . . I laid perfectly still as Bo Jangles peeked out of the leaves above me. *"I smell it too, Tanya. They are about two blocks away. So, stay quiet."*

Nodding at my feline companion, I stood, quiet as I could, picked up my crossbow, and took one step over to the tree I had just been laying under. I watched the nearby street as the stench of undead bodies got stronger. "I thought you said there wasn't anything around for miles? How many are there, Bo?" I whispered while planning the quickest way back to our hideout.

The cat lying above me ignored my first question as I saw her tail slowly move back and forth in the tree, her eyes fixated on something ahead of us. *"Three, Tanya."* I heard that voice sound in my head and let out a quick breath of relief. Three? I could handle three. No problem. *"Uh, Tanya, they have a live person with them. I think it might be an alien."*

Glancing back up into the tree, I could just make out that large fur ball, her tail now still, her ears laid back on her head, watching the undead moving down the street from her vantage point. I wondered for a fleeting second if this was another one of Bo's jokes, but I could see that she was intent on watching the bodies and wasn't playing around. This was something different and, in this world, at this time, different was always deadly.

Focusing back on the street, within a few seconds, I saw that the cat was right. There were three undead walking down the road with a smaller fourth person tethered behind them. They were shuffling along pulling the being behind them as though it was a reluctant dog. Concentrating on trying to identify the person, Bo's voice startled me. *"I think we should go home now, Tanya, and leave these creatures to do whatever they will with the alien. It's starting to get late and we need to get back home before dark."*

Glancing up at the cat, I saw her unblinking yellow eyes staring down at me and then looked out at the four figures moving down the street. "Alien? Damn. No, we take the zombies out and then we see if the alien has any useful information for us. Like why the undead are taking prisoners instead of just eating them? We still have enough daylight left," I whispered as I raised my crossbow and aimed at the lead zombie shuffling down the street.

"I think this is a bad idea, Tanya. We can't be outside if he decides to visit tonight." That voice from above rebuked with just the smallest trace of fear.

"Yeah, I sorta think it's a bad idea too, Bo, but keep the alien from escaping while I deal with the undead. Besides anything new in this world isn't good for us," I whispered. I hit the trigger of the crossbow. Cocked it, hit the trigger again. Cocked and hit the trigger a third time and watched as all three of my bolts hit the undead in the center of their foreheads. Booyeah, three for three. Damn, I'm a great shot for a fifteen-year-old if I do say so myself. Yeah, I know zombies aren't that quick, but hell now they won't be moving at all.

Walking over to the four bodies on the ground, three with bolts sticking out of their heads and the fourth with a large feline fur ball sitting in the middle of its chest, I laughed as I checked the zombies' bodies to make sure that they were truly dead then walked over to where Bo and the alien lay.

"I stopped it from escaping, Tanya."

"Yeah, I can see that, Bo, but did you have to kill it?"

The cat looked up at me, blinked, then looked back down at the alien it was perched on, then back up at me with a confused look on her face. *"It's still alive."*

"My mistake, Bo. I guess with all that weight sitting on its chest it was hard to see if it was actually breathing," I laughed. I took in the alien face that wasn't all that different from mine except for the slightly pointed ears, tiny whiskers and a nose that matched Bo Jangles'.

Bo blinked again then huffed as she launched herself off the alien. She scampered toward the trees my laughter following her as her voice rang in my head. *"Fat, am I? Well, just you wait and see what kind of surprise I leave inside your boots tomorrow morning. Call me fat. Well, I'll just deposit a little of that 'fat' somewhere you won't like . . ."*

Her voice stopped as she jumped into the nearest tree and disappeared to sulk. "Oh, come on, Bo. I was only joking," I laughed. Waiting a few seconds to see if she would come back, I glanced down at the unconscious alien that was still lying on the ground. Seeing that it didn't look like it was going anywhere soon, I turned and walked back to the trees where my friend had disappeared. I really didn't want to wake up tomorrow morning with one of her 'surprises' lying in wait for me. They tended to be rather large and smelly. One of the reasons that I had abandoned a cat box in the house and made her use the outside for her bodily functions. "Bo? Bo Jangles, stop goofing around and get back here. Come on. I was only kidding, Bo."

Hearing a tiny huff of annoyance in my head I thought she was some distance away and shrugged thinking that when she got out of her funk she would be back. So, I turned my attention to other matters. Like how to get the alien back home if she wasn't awake.

Walking over I saw part of the problem was solved as the alien's eyes were open and blinking up at the afternoon sun. "Well, well, I see we're awake." It slowly turned its head toward me and gave me a quick insolent once over then went back to staring up at the sky. Well, now, that was rather rude if I do say so myself.

"You got a name?" Nothing but silence once more. In fact, I didn't even get that look again as though I wasn't important enough to even take any notice of, though it did sit up. The alien glanced at the three zombies I had killed with the same indifference it had shown me then stared down at the ground between its legs.

Walking over to the alien, I pointed my weapon in its general direction. "Look it's getting late and I need to get home. So, you have two choices. The first choice is that I shoot you and leave you for what comes out at night. A snack like you, I figure they'll leave me alone for a couple of days." I looked over the smaller alien and laughed, "Then again, maybe one day since there isn't much of you to eat." The alien stared at me, fury darkening its face before it went back to staring at the ground. "Or, second choice, you start talking and I take you back with me to my house. Either way, I could care less."

"Just kill it, Tanya. Better yet, just wound it and let a shadow kill it. It's not smart enough to understand you. You aren't going to get anything out of it." That voice rang in my head as I took a step back from the alien and glanced at the cat that was strutting up to us, her tail waving high in the air.

"I see you're over your snit," I laughed as the cat came up and sat next to me and started to lick her paws.

"I don't know what snit you're talking about. Besides, it's almost dark and I'm hungry. So, kill it or wound it and let's get home. You need to do your job and feed me."

Looking down at Bo Jangles, I sighed. "You know, we really need to sit down and talk over what you think my job is and isn't around here, cat."

"Whatever. I'm a cat. You really think I care, girl? Just kill it already. I'm starved."

Looking over at the alien, I sighed. "My friend here just wants me to kill you so she can go get her dinner, or she suggests that we wound you and leave you for the shadows to have fun with." Nothing but silence again from the alien. "Fine, Bo's probably right and you're too stupid to know our language anyway so I won't get anything useful out of you," I mumbled as I raised the crossbow.

"Suzu."

"Excuse me?"

The alien looked up at me, eyes flashing that anger again and snarled, "I said my name is Suzu. I understand your crude language."

"Well, now, that wasn't so hard, was it? And just to let you know it's not smart to insult the language of the one holding the weapon," I laughed as the alien glared up at me.

Bo Jangles snorted. *"I still say kill it. No good is going to come of this if you keep it alive. You know he isn't going to be happy if you bring that thing home with you. You don't need a pet. You have me, Tanya."*

"Chill out, Bo. If it tries anything I'll feed it to the night shadows, okay?" I snapped back at the cat. She knew I didn't like talking about him.

The cat's laugh was nasty as the alien looked between us puzzled as I had what looked like a one-way conversation with Bo. "Are you talking to that mangy feline Earth creature?"

Bo Jangles stood up, her fur ruffling in anger as she snarled, *"I'll show you mangy . . . you flea-bitten, two-legged . . ."*

"Chill, Bo," I said as I stepped in front of the mass of pissed off cat and turned toward the alien. "Uhm, not a good idea to make her mad, and yes, I can talk to her as she talks back to me."

"How . . . I mean when . . ."

"Listen, Suzu, I'm sure you have lots of questions as I have a million of my own, but right now we need to get a move on and get back to my house before night falls. So how about you stand up and we get moving?"

The alien held up her tied hands, as though needing help, and I took a step forward before Bo stepped in front of me and blocked me from going any closer. *"What the hell do you think you're doing, girl?"*

The alien watched this exchange as I turned red-faced and raised my crossbow. "Nice try, Suzu. Do that again and I'll just kill you and save myself any future problems."

The alien shrugged and with a sly smile hopped off the ground without any effort. Taking a few steps back, I nodded and smiled back at the alien as I pointed up the street. "That way. Move."

An hour later it was nearing dark and I was getting a little worried. I wasn't the only one. I could tell Bo Jangles was nervous by the twitches of her tail and the way she kept sniffing the air. The trip back to our hideout should have only taken us half that time to get there, but after a few minutes of walking, I could see that the alien must have been wounded as Suzu was limping. Slowing us down.

Suzu must have picked up on our agitation as the alien started to look warily around the area and tried to pick up the pace a bit more. A few minutes later, I caught sight of our home and breathed a deep sigh of relief. "Over there." I pointed to a worn looking eight-foot high double-ringed chain-linked fences, each with a roll of barb wire strung along its top.

"Nice," Suzu muttered as we stopped and I unlocked and opened the gates and we walked through to the six-foot wood fence just beyond.

Reaching down to open the next gate, I caught a flash of fur as Bo jumped over the fence and into the yard beyond. "Show off," I laughed as I followed the alien through the next gate and turned locking it behind us.

The alien looked around at the yard before the house and nodded. To one side stood a small greenhouse. On the other side was an area that held a small garden now lying dormant for the coming winter. The two-story house in front of us was built into the side of a hill and made of concrete with only one entry. "Lucky you found this fort."

Looking around, I nodded. "Yeah, luck had nothing to do with it. My daddy and I lived here before you guys decided to come and try to take our world from us," I said as I looked up as the sky darkened. "Come on, we need to get inside before full dark."

The alien looked back at the gate and then at me. "I don't think the undead of this world could get in here that easy."

"Yeah, well, there are worse things out after dark than zombies," I said as I pushed the alien toward the house.

We stopped at the edge of the concrete building and looked up at the second story concrete decking that clung to the side. Bo Jangles' furry face looked down on us from the open gateway as I heard her voice in my head once again. *"So, the magic word is?"*

"Bo Jangles, quit messing around. We don't have time for this." The cat stretched and stood up flipping her tail at me as she turned and disappeared. Seconds later a metal ladder unrolled, the bottom landing at our feet.

The alien started to reach for the ladder when I nudged her with the tip of my crossbow. "Hold it. I'll go up first. You go stand over by the side there," I said pointing to a corner of the house.

A tiny flicker of fear crossed her face then fled as she moved to where I had pointed. "You changed your mind and you're going to leave me down here for these shadow creatures?"

Laughing at the idea, I reached out and scampered up the ladder. Getting to the top, I turned and looked down on the alien. "If I had wanted to leave you for them I would have done it outside my yard. I have no intention of drawing them in here if I can help it. Now get up here, we don't have much time."

The alien awkwardly climbed the ladder and was soon standing on my front porch. "Now what?"

Reaching over and shutting the gate, I pointed to a tiny handle next to the alien. "Now you crank that handle so the ladder comes up and we get inside before it gets full dark."

The alien didn't say a word, but looked down at the fences around my home, at the ladder, and then back at me. "You really think something can get up here?"

"Oh, I know something can get up here. Now start cranking or I will leave you out here to find out what made those marks." The alien glanced at a set of claw marks gouged into the concrete walls, paled, and then vigorously started to crank on the handle reeling in the ladder. Yeah, I had thought the sight of those marks would change her mind. Bo seemed to have thought so too as I heard her laughter ring inside my head.

With the right motivation, it didn't take the alien long to get the ladder rolled up and stowed away. Once it was secure, I finally got us inside just as the last rays of the sun dipped below the trees.

Heoheska 39th Light Mobile Scouts - Outside Mt. Vernon, Washington:

Keiko walked around the perimeter of the small camp in a foul mood as he checked each of the guards to be sure that they weren't asleep. After last night, he would kill any Heoheska warrior that even hinted at not being fully alert.

As he moved through the night he thought back on the hellish year that he, Nasreer, and Suzu had spent on this cursed world. How after the three of them had escaped Seattle they had moved north picking up other Heoheska warriors along the way. Many of them, like the three survivors, leftovers from units the packs of undead humans had avenged themselves on.

Many of those warriors had died during the year, Nasreer included, going down under the hands and teeth of these undead humans or other things that roamed this planet. No, that wasn't what had Keiko in such a foul mood. No, death for a Heoheska warrior was nothing new. It was the sudden disappearance of his medic, Suzu, two nights ago that had him so worked up.

There was something strange about it. It wasn't like she was killed by the undead humans. If it had been an attack more Heoheska than Suzu would have died that night. It was almost as though something had come and spirited her away from the camp.

Keiko arrived at the last guard post and his thoughts changed from wondering about his companions. The young Heoheska warriors manning the post were a second slow in challenging him. A loud bellow and the sounds of blows rang through the still night air.

Chapter 4

Slamming the heavy metal door behind us, I turned the locking wheel and slid the three steel bars across it before I could finally take a breath and relax. Turning, I pointed to a chair. "Sit over there while I get these windows shut.

The alien slumped down into the chair while Bo hopped up on the table next to it and stared, her golden eyes never even blinking. *"He isn't going to like this you know, Tanya."*

"Yeah, yeah, you said that before, Bo. Now shut up about him. Hopefully, he stays away," I said as I shut the two windows and slid their locking bars into place.

"Yeah, fat chance of that happening."

"Uh, what?" the alien asked watching me go through my routine of closing up for the night.

"Nothing, I was talking to Bo," I snipped as I walked over and pulled a knife. Reaching down, I sliced the rope tying her hands together. Explaining everything Bo said to the alien was going to get tiring fast.

The alien glanced between the two of us and snickered, echoing my own thoughts. "Well, that will get tiring fast."

"Don't like it, you can always leave." That wiped the smirk off the alien's face as she rubbed her wrists. "Yeah, didn't think so."

"So just how does this thing talk to you? I didn't hear it say anything to you," the alien asked nodding at the cat sitting next to it.

"I hear Bo Jangles in my head when she talks. In fact, that's how we found her just after the bombs went off. She was the last of her litter and crying for her mother so I tracked down her pitiful cries."

"Hey, watch who you call pitiful there, short stuff." I laughed as Bo huffed and hopped off the table flipping her tail in the alien's face in the process. She walked over to me and sat down once again giving the alien her evil cat eye.

"Who is we?"

My laughter died as I looked over at Suzu confused by her question. "What? Who are we? What are you talking about?"

"You said, 'we found her.' Is there someone else here? Someone in charge?"

"No, there isn't anyone else here now. I'm in charge all by my lonesome, and it was my daddy and I that found Bo Jangles just after the blasts that killed the cities just for your information."

"Okay, but where . . ."

"NO MORE QUESTIONS!" I yelled as I felt a burning rage well up in me. I grabbed the focus stone hanging around my neck and took that rage and concentrated it into my other hand. Turning, I threw a ball of flame into the fireplace lighting the wood and paper that I had set up just this morning.

It was quiet in the room except for the slight crackle of the flame as the paper and wood fed the fire. The anger inside me cooled from that quick burst of release. *"Temper, temper, Tanya."* Bo stared at me concern on her face. Of course, she had been accidentally on the wrong end of a few of my temper tantrums when I first started to throw fire.

"How did you do that?" the alien whispered a little bit of fright and awe slipping into her voice.

Ignoring the alien, I bent down and rubbed between my friend's ears as I whispered, "You of all people should not be warning me about temper, Bo." I slipped the stone on its leather cord inside my shirt and felt the warm magic residue on my skin.

"Human, how did you do that? That thing with the fire?" the alien's strident voice now demanding an answer.

Looking up, my eyes flashing with a fire that matched the one behind me, I snarled as the stone in my shirt grew hotter. "You and your damn bombs are what caused me to be able to do that . . . that magic."

"Calm down, Tanya, before you burn your shirt up."

"Magic?"

I took Bo's suggestion and took a deep calming breath before replying as I felt the stone grow cooler. "Yeah, you know, causing things to appear out of thin air. For me it's fire."

"I don't understand. I mean the bombs the leaders set off were supposed to wipe your species off this planet, not give you this magic or bring your dead back to life."

"Oh, you don't know the half of what those damn bombs did to my race, or for that matter most biological life on this world." I stopped talking as I felt another wash of heat start to fill me up and glanced down at the small puddle of blueish blood that was gathering below the alien's boot. "You're bleeding. I mean I think you're bleeding. Is that the color of your blood?"

The alien gazed down at the puddle of fluid and shrugged. "Guess I am bleeding."

"Right," I said standing and walking over to a cupboard and started to rummage through it looking for my first aid kit. "Get that armor off and I'll patch you up."

Hearing the rustle of cloth and metal, I didn't pay much attention to the alien as I was looking for that damn elusive first aid kit. Oh, there it is. Grabbing the kit, I caught Bo's laughter ring in my head. *"Oh, Tanya,"* she sang out, and I turned the first aid kit now in my hand.

My mouth dropped open at the sight of the naked alien standing there leaning against the table. "Uhm, you're a girl."

The alien looked down at herself and shrugged as she looked back at me. "Yes, I'm a female. All medics are."

"Yeah, but you have four . . . I mean you're not as . . . uhm, furry as I thought you would be," I stammered then stopped took a deep breath and shook my head at her. "What I meant was that I wanted you to take your armor off not everything else too."

Suzu looked down at the pile of armor at her feet and shrugged again. "We don't wear anything under the armor. It's basically a one-piece outfit. You either have it on or you're, well, like this," she said as she swept her hand over her body.

Turning around, I grabbed the nearest clothes off the counter and threw them in the general direction of the girl. "Okay then. We look about the same size in most areas. How about you throw these on and then I'll look at your leg," I said peering at the floor.

Suzu shrugged then rummaged through the clothes until she found a pair of shorts and a tee to wear. "Is there a problem with me being naked? I mean we are both females. I mean, you are a human female, right? So . . ." Her voice trailed off as she looked me over.

Looking up, I shook my head as I felt myself flush again. "Yes, I'm female, and it's just that humans aren't used to just . . . standing around with no clothes on is all. Or, at least, most of us aren't."

The alien sat down in the chair and nodded as she looked at me. "Sorry, I will try to remember that. It's just that for us Heoheska if we aren't in our armor . . . well, you know."

"Yeah, that's fine. In fact, more than I really need to know. Now, let's look at that leg of yours," I said as I grabbed another chair and had Suzu lay her injured leg across it. I knelt next to the chair and saw that she had a long cut running up the outside of her leg that didn't look too good.

As I stared down at the cut, the alien flexed her leg in pain and I thought I could see a flash of white. The room spun a little as I felt the blood drain from my face. "Are you alright, human? You look a little pale."

Standing up fast, I grabbed the table as I felt a wave of nausea wash over me again. Oh, that was so not such a good idea. "Uh, yeah, I'm fine. I just don't do well with . . ."

"Yeah, I can see that. If you don't mind, I'll just take care of this myself then since I am a medic."

I gulped and nodded as I passed over the first aid kit to Suzu. "Sure, have at it."

The medic set the first aid kit on the table then looked through it for a few minutes before sighing and looking back up at me. "This is not a good combat medic kit. Could you hand me that pack down there?"

Nodding, I reached down and picked up a small grey pack and started to hand it to Suzu when I hesitated. She smiled. "I promise you there are no weapons in the pack, human."

"It's Tanya," I said as I handed the pack over. Bo hopped up on the table and stared down at the wound with some interest.

"What?"

"My name. My name is Tanya, not human."

"Alright, Tanya." She chuckled as she moved my first aid kit aside and opened her own medic bag. She was quiet as she rummaged through then brought out a syringe and popped the cap off a long, long needle. Without hesitation, she stuck that needle into her wound and pushed the plunger.

I felt another wave of dizziness wash over me and I turned and stumbled into the kitchen, mumbling, "I think I'll make us some dinner." I heard Suzu's quiet laughter in the room as Bo's rang in my head. Damn cat always found it amusing just because I got a little woozy at the sight of blood.

Standing there in the kitchen, looking around, I tried to figure out what to make. I heard a soft chuckle from my feline friend. *"Oh, cool, Tanya. You should come and see this. She is stitching it all up herself. Damn, bet that hurts. Ask her if that really hurts, girl."* I ignored the comments and walked over to the cupboard and pulled out a couple of MREs and a can of cat food.

"I'm done now, human." I heard from the living room as I opened the can and one of the MRE bags.

"It's Tanya, not human, at least, if you want to stay here tonight and get fed that is," I said as I walked into the next room and handed the open bag to Suzu. "Traitor," I whispered at Bo and slid the open can of cat food toward her.

"Hey, aren't you going to put that in my bowl?"

I chuckled at her indignant voice. "Oh, I might faint since I still feel woozy. So, guess the can will have to do." I heard her grumble as she buried her head in the can, and I chose to ignore where she told me I could shove the can since that would hurt.

"What is this stuff?"

Looking over at Suzu, I could see that she had already opened the main meal pouch and was digging into with wild abandon. "It's called lima beans and ham."

She nodded and then dug into the pouch for more of the concoction inside. I shuddered in disgust as she licked her fingers and smiled. "That is so much better than our field rations."

I just nodded and smiled as I finished off my spaghetti MRE. "Well, that's good cause I have plenty of that type left." I gathered up our stuff and threw it in the trash when we were both done before I turned back to the alien and sighed. "What are we going to do with you now that I have you here? I need to get some sleep."

Suzu gazed at me as Bo interjected her two cents into the matter. *"See. I told you, you should have killed her out there in the woods. I mean any creature that likes lima beans and ham has no . . ."*

"Shut up, Bo, this is serious."

Suzu glanced over at Bo who yawned just then showing off her razor-sharp teeth and then back at me. "I take it she doesn't trust me."

"I don't trust you, Suzu."

Suzu got a solemn look on her face as she whispered, "I give you my warrior's oath that I will not harm you or your pet . . ."

"Pet my furry rear-end . . ."

". . . while I am with you."

"Okay."

"Okay? That's it? Okay?"

"WHAT!?! Have you gone out of your ever-loving mind, girl?"

I smiled at the two of them and nodded. "Yeah, okay. Are you telling me that your oath is worthless?"

I watched Suzu's face go dark as her eyes blazed with anger. "A Heoheska will die before they break their oath."

I shrugged and pointed to a cot in the corner. "Okay, then you sleep there."

The anger died in her eyes as she glanced over at the cot and then at me. Slowly she got up making sure that she put as little weight as she could on her wounded leg and limped over to the bed. As she lay down, I did a quick check on the doors and windows and then headed for my own bed. "Oh, and Suzu . . ."

"Yes?"

"If you hear anything in the night. No matter what do not open any of the doors or windows." She lay there looking at me then I saw her glance at the door and nod. "Good night then," I whispered as I lay back on the thick pillow that was one of my prized possessions.

I felt Bo hop up on the end of the bed and settle down at the end of the bed with a huff. *"Well, I for one am not going to sleep, Tanya."* I smiled as the fire died and the room went dark. After a few minutes, everyone settled down and I quietly reached under my pillow and brought out Miss Sassy from her hiding place. I cuddled the old patched doll that I had had since I was a baby and I closed my eyes.

Chapter 5

Opening my eyes, it took me a second to adjust to the darkness that was lit only by the few remaining coals from the fireplace. I tried to figure out why I had awakened when I heard scratching at the door and a whispered 'Tanya.'

Ever so slowly, I crawled out of bed Miss Sassy grasped in my hands and moved across the room. Sitting down on the cold floor by the door, I leaned against it as the scratching stopped. It was quiet for a few seconds when I heard a hissing whisper. "Tanya, my love?"

"Yes."

"Did you like the present that I sent you?"

Glancing over at where Suzu lay I saw that she was still sleeping, but leaned even closer to the door and whispered, "You sent her with the zombies?"

"Yes."

"But how? I mean the undead . . ."

"We are learning to control them. Control the undead. So that we can fight the invaders and take back our world."

"We?"

A slight hiss that could be a laugh then that whisper again. "Yes. There are more of . . . more of my kind. More of what I have become in this world as there are other . . . other things . . . other creatures out there."

I clutched the doll tighter to my chest and shivered. "Okay. But why did you send her to me?"

"I sent her to you because I know you are lonely, Daughter. I will try to protect you for the aliens are moving this way, but you must be prepared to move if I cannot stop them."

A few tears fell from my eyes and ran down the door as I crushed my doll even harder. "Thank you, Daddy." I sat there waiting for a response, but only silence remained on the other side of the door. After a few minutes, I wiped the tears from my face and quietly crawled back into bed. I had just settled back under the warm covers when I heard Bo Jangles let out a loud snore.

Suzu peeked out of barely opened eyes as she watched the scene at the door. She lay quietly trying to make out the whispered voices as the young Earth girl sat with tears dripping down her face. Daddy? The human had called whatever was on the other side of the door her daddy. As Tanya pulled herself off the floor and crawled back into bed, the medic wondered just what had her species done to the humans on this world and whether it would come back to bite them in the ass.

The hand covering my mouth woke me up and as my eyes opened, I stared back at the alien standing over me. "Don't make a sound. There is something outside trying to get into the door," Suzu whispered.

Lying there listening to the silence in the room for a few seconds I soon heard a scratching sound at the door and the ringing of Bo's voice in my head. *"Tanya, let me in. It's cold out here this morning. I want my litter box back inside."*

Sitting up, I pushed Suzu's hand off my mouth and left her with a puzzled look on her face as I stalked over to the door. "It's Bo."

I removed the bars from the door, opening it just enough for the cat to barely squeeze by before closing it again. *"Thanks,"* the cat said as she sauntered in and hopped up on the table. Spinning around twice in a circle and sitting down in a huff. *"So, what's for breakfast, Tanya? Come on you're up and you need to feed me before I waste away to nothing."*

Shaking my head at the cat, I thought it would be a long while before she ever wasted away. I glanced over at my bed and lunged as Suzu picked up Miss Sassy with a look of curiosity on her face. "What is this?"

Grabbing the doll out her hand, I shoved it under my pillow. I could feel the stone I wore heating up against my skin as my anger flared. "What the hell . . ."

"I'm sorry, huma . . . Tanya. I was just curious what it was."

I glared down at the alien. "It's none of your business. Now get off my bed. That cot is your bed. This is my bed. So, keep your butt on yours and off mine. Got me, alien?"

She stood up as she threw a quick glance at my pillow then at the cat sitting on the table. "Look, I'm sorry, okay?"

"Tanya, it's just a doll. Anyways . . ." I threw a dirty look at Bo. She hopped off the table, laughing. *"Alien, you're on your own."*

Turning back to Suzu, I took a deep breath. "Don't touch my stuff. Alright?"

"Sure, yeah, no problem."

"Fine," I snarled as I opened the windows and then walked into the kitchen to get us all some breakfast.

"So, uhm, how did your pet get outside?" I heard the voice behind me and I startled a little. I glanced over my shoulder and saw Suzu inches away from me. Man, I might have to put a bell on her. She's as quiet as Bo . . . "Tanya, I asked how did it get outside?"

I heard Bo grumble from the other room. *"It has a name you fleabag from another world."*

"What? Sorry, I was drifting off for a second. What did you say?"

Suzu took a deep breath and shook her head. "For the third time, I asked how that thing got outside?" I thought you said it was too dangerous to go out?"

"There's a tiny trap door in the roof that she can barely squeeze through. She can get out, but not in. That way nothing can find its way in here."

"I just have one question."

"Only one, Suzu?"

She shrugged. "Yeah what is this place?"

"It was my daddy's and my home. He was this crazy old survivalist. At least that was what people always called him. He prepared this place for the end of the world. I guess he wasn't so crazy after all."

"What about your mother?"

"She left a long time ago. When I was five, I think. She moved down to Seattle. Guess she didn't quite share in my father's beliefs that little green men were going to destroy the world."

I watched as the alien looked down at herself then back up at me. "I'm not green."

Laughing, I threw her an MRE bag as I went to open a can of cat food for Bo Jangles. "Don't worry about it. It's just an Earth expression."

Heoheska 5th Mobile Light Armored Scout - Outside Bellingham, WA

The eight-man crew of the light-armored scout had been traveling all day in their vehicles glad to be away from the task of killing zombies in the city south of them. After a year of neglect and bad weather, the roads around this part of the country were torn up causing the vehicles to move slowly through this country. The warriors were more than happy when their leader called a halt for the night. They were less than thrilled when the sub-captain posted guards. Their section sergeant grumbled for a few minutes to his officer, but each warrior was a veteran that knew when to argue with an officer and when to just do what they were told.

As the sun rose over the mountains, the Heoheska sub-captain opened his eyes and tried to move his arms and legs. He struggled for several minutes against the barbed wire that held him to the side of his armored vehicle until it cut even deeper into his flesh. Fresh blood flowed from the abraded skin to mix with the old. The buzz of flies droned in his ears as his head slowly sunk down to his chest the dead eyes of his men staring accusingly up at him. His mind wandered back to the nightmare that had been last night.

"Captain? Captain Letine, time to wake up," the harsh hissing voice in front of him whispered.

Letine startled awake and found himself tied to the side of a vehicle. Desperately, he fought against the restraints holding him until the pain from the wire cutting through his skin made him stop. Breathing hard, he focused on the dark shadow that stood in front of him. A shadow darker than the surrounding night except for a pair of cold white eyes that stared back at him. "Who are you and what have you done to my men?"

The shadow moved aside and the sub-captain could see his men huddled on the ground bound together. Scattered around the warriors, Letine saw a large number of the undead standing silently as their putrid odor finally assaulted his nose. "See? I have done nothing to your men, Captain. Yet. And as for what I am? Why I am of your own making."

"What do you want? I don't know what the hell you're talking about."

"I want you to tell your leaders that they will go no further than this spot. That anything north of this area is off limits."

Letine tried to laugh, but it came out half-croak, half-fear induced sob. "We are Heoheska warriors . . . if you think . . ."

"Please, Sub-Captain, look down at your men and at yourself. I have taken your whole unit on my own. Just think what I can do with others of my kind."

The sub-captain shook his head from side to side as he whispered, "No, I . . . "

"Feed, but leave the heads."

At that command, the sub-captain watched in growing horror as the undead fell upon his bound men. Their screams filled the night air as the zombies ripped armor off the warriors and reached for tender flesh with their hands and teeth.

Letine fought against the restraints that held him, sobbing in frustration and anger as he watched his men torn to shreds by the undead creatures. Ten minutes after the last scream echoed in the night there was nothing left of his warriors except for a few scraps lying here and there and, surprisingly, his men's heads. The sub-captain could see the terror that was etched in the now dead eyes staring accusingly back at him from the ground. Mouths gaped open in pleading, silent screams. The shadow in front of him had complete control of the undead.

The sub-captain gave up fighting and let his head fall to his chest as he sobbed, "I swear by my men's lives that I will find you and kill you. You shall never escape . . ."

A dark hiss sounded, cutting off his tirade. It took a second for the captain to realize that it was laughter. "No, my dear Captain, that will not happen." The shadow turned away and walked over to the undead that once again stood quietly in the night. As the sub-captain watched the shadow reached inside one of the zombie's mouths and wiped a finger inside it.

He watched, puzzled, as the shadow turned and slithered back to him. "What are you doing?"

The darkness stood before him and slowly brought his hand up to the gaping wound on the bound alien's wrist and stuck his finger deep within it drawing a hiss of pain. "Why, my dear Captain, I am repaying your kind for what they did to my world." That hissing laughter sounded as the shadow pushed his finger deeper in the wound and wiggled it around.

"WHAT ARE YOU DOING? WHAT'RE YOU TALKING ABOUT?" The sub-captain screamed as he renewed the fight against the ties that held him to the vehicle.

The shadow stopped what he was doing and slowly pulled his finger from the alien's wrist and stepped back so that all the sub-captain could see were those cold white eyes. "It is simple, Captain, I have made you one of the undead. You see, I have found that if one of your kind is bitten by the undead then you will turn."

The sub-captain hung limply as he whispered, "Turn?"

"Yes, you will become one of them. You will change into the undead."

"NO! This can't be. Humans are different from us. We . . ."

42

The shadow shook his head and laughed. "Oh, Captain, I'm afraid it is very true and is happening. You see, I have conducted some experiments and have found that there is a virus in the zombie's blood that affects your race as well as humans."

"But how?"

"How, Captain? I guess someone on your world screwed up, didn't they? So now I and others like me will infect as many of your kind as we can and when you return to your world yours will suffer the fate that my world has."

"I'll tell them. I'll make them kill me so that . . ."

"Oh, Captain, by the time they find you, you will be raving mad from the virus. And as for killing you, well, anyone that comes in contact with your body, whether you're dead or alive, will become infected. See you shall only be the first of many." The captain moaned. The virus already starting to course through his body as the shadow moved closer and whispered, "Remember Captain, no one may cross this point. Above all else, you must remember to tell them this." The captain moaned again as the shadow moved off into the night the undead slowly, reluctantly, leaving the promise of fresh blood and flesh behind.

Chapter 6

"So, what are we going to do now?" the alien asked as she licked the last of the lima bean and ham mixture off her fingers. Shuddering a little at the sight of her licking that tasteless god-awful mess off her fingers, I shrugged and finished off the last of my eggs and bacon. Suzu stopped dipping her fingers in the bag and looked at me. "What do you usually do? I mean you don't just sit around here all day doing nothing, do you?"

Reaching over and grabbing the bag out of her hand, I tossed both of them into the trash can and started back into the main room of the house. Bo was stretched out on the floor basking in the warm sunbeam that was filtering through the open window coverings. Hearing the quiet shuffle of the alien's feet behind me, I turned and snarled at her, "What do you want?"

She stopped then took a step back as she saw the stone that I wore glow against my skin. "Nothing, Tanya. I don't want anything. I was just making conversation was all. I was curious about how you survived all this time on your own."

Taking a few deep breaths to calm myself, which I seem to be doing a lot since this alien had fallen into my life, I sat down and started to put my boots on. "Sorry, I'm just used to it being just Bo and me around. I'm not used to talking with anyone else."

"How long have you been alone, human?"

"Hey, what am I chopped liver? You would think we don't . . . zzzz."

I finished putting on my boots and started tying them giving me a second to think back. "I guess it was about a month after 'The Day' that my daddy left me."

"Left you?"

"Uhm, Tanya, he might not like you telling the alien about this stuff."

Looking over at the large cat that lay on the floor, I shook my head and smiled. "He told me last night that he sent her to me, Bo. So, don't sweat the small stuff."

"Dealing with him is never small stuff, girl," the cat said blinking her eyes before she laid her head back down in the warm sunbeam and snored again.

The alien looked between the two of us, puzzled. "Who sent who to you?"

I sighed. "My daddy sent you to me because he said I was lonely." I heard the cat snort and mumble something about being chopped liver again before dozing off as I watched Suzu's face darken with anger.

"You mean to tell me this father of yours leaves you and then sends me to you like . . . like . . ." she pointed to Bo still lying on the floor, "a pet to keep you company." The cat's quiet laughter rang in my ears as Suzu sputtered.

"Yeah, something like that."

Suzu hopped to her feet, anger flushing her face. "Let me tell you something, human. I am not anyone's pet. Human or otherwise. Got me?"

Shrugging, I reached down into a pile of clothes and threw a long-sleeved shirt and pants at the alien. "Whatever. It's not like I asked him to bring you here. So, don't get mad at me. Now put those on and we'll head out."

Suzu glanced down at her clothes then back at me. "And why should I wear these human clothes instead of my armor?"

Shrugging again, I picked up my daypack and headed to the kitchen to pack some supplies for the day. "I could care less what you wear, Suzu. Of course, if we run into any humans they're most likely to shoot at anyone wearing your armor first and then ask questions later. So, suit yourself."

The alien threw a look at her armor then at the clothes in her hands. She smiled at me as she tossed the clothes on the floor and started to strip. Yeah, we were going to have to make some rules about personal space and modesty when we got back from our little scout.

Bo's drowsy snicker followed me into the storage area and, for a second, I thought about 'forgetting' to bring any food for the cat but dismissed that idea as it wouldn't be worth the complaining I would hear from her all day long. That is if I could pry her away from the warm spot she was lying in.

By the time I was done getting stuff together Suzu was decent and had her boots on ready to go. Bo was still lying in the middle of the floor enjoying one of the rare sunbeams that filtered into the room. I reached inside the pack and threw the alien a belt wrapped around a knife.

That brought the cat off the floor in a rush. *"ARE YOU OUT OF YOUR EVER-FRICKING LOVING MIND, GIRL?!"*

I glanced at Bo then at Suzu as she slid the long blade out of its sheath and tested the balance and weight of the knife. "I figured you can't go out there without a weapon. I won't give you a long-range weapon right now, but I won't take you out there unarmed either."

"Thanks."

"No problem. Think you can handle it?"

The alien slid the knife back into the sheath and put the belt around her waist. "Women on my planet aren't classified as warriors, but medics are taught the fundamentals of simple weapons. So yes, I can handle it."

"Okay . . . uhm, just out of curiosity how old are you, Suzu?"

She cocked her head to the side gazing at me for a second then looked down at her boots. "I am fifteen years old, Tanya."

"Fifteen? You're my age? They let you join the army at fifteen?"

Suzu's laughter bounced off the walls of the room as I tried to figure out what was so funny. She shook her head at my puzzled look. "Oh, human, there is no letting someone join our forces. Everyone from the age of five is taken from their family and trained in our military."

"Everyone?"

A depressed looked crossed her face and that fast it was gone. "Yes, everyone."

"What if someone isn't cut out to be in the military?"

Her head dropped and I thought I saw a tear fall from her face as she whispered, "Then they are killed like my baby sister was."

"Damn. That's brutal."

"That is life on my planet. We are ruled by the military. Every facet of our lives and beliefs are geared toward the warrior's life and death. Women are only allowed to function as medics or as clerical staff until they reach the age of twenty."

"Then what happens?"

"Then we are expected to breed warriors for our planet."

I stood and looked at Suzu. Shaking my head, I marveled at that thought for a second. "Damn. I thought my world was backward with how they treat women. Ain't nothing compared to yours."

Heoheska 3rd Scout Squad – Outside Bellingham, WA.

The five warriors in the unit moved down the side of the road, not a whisper of sound coming from any of them as they scanned the area for any danger. They were, in their sergeant's opinion, on a garbage detail looking for a missing unit that was supposed to be just ahead of the main column. It was probably just some fouled up communications or someone asleep at the radio. There was no real reason why they had been moving since before daylight to find one 'lost' patrol.

The leader raised one hand, seeing movement to his front, and the other four warriors dropped to their knees taking a defensive posture around him. The sergeant squinted in the early morning light then relaxed as he saw the sixth man of his unit rapidly approach.

The sergeant kept kneeling, taking a well-deserved break from the long march they had endured since three this morning when his commander had kicked him awake and ordered him to find the missing unit.

As the sergeant rested, his mind wandered over the conversation that he had had with his unit commander, a little pissant sub-lieutenant just fresh out of officer school. Granted, no Heoheska warrior is at his best at three in the morning but that was no reason for the child to be in such a mood.

Making them walk all this way because he wanted to use the unit's armored vehicle to have some alone time with the medic. That was another sore point with him. Sending his unit into the field without a medic. The sergeant decided that when he and his men got back to the unit it was time to put that damn child in his place, officer or not.

The running warrior finally reached his companions drawing the sergeant from his musings and skidded to a halt in front of them. Going to one knee, he tried to catch his breath. After a few seconds, the sergeant barked, "Well? Anything ahead of us?"

The warrior nodded as he tried to catch his breath while glancing back over his shoulder. The sergeant looked to the front and didn't see anything coming after his solider, but noticed that the warrior was pale. He gave him a few more minutes to catch his breath then in a quieter voice demanded, "Did you find them?"

The private gulped then nodded. "What's left of them, Sergeant."

"Tell me what you found."

"I saw their vehicles and one body. The rest . . . the rest . . . they're in a line . . . and looking toward . . ."

The sergeant saw the warrior go paler and took ahold of the man's shoulder and gave it a quick shake. "Get ahold of yourself and quit acting like a female in heat. What did you see?"

"An undead feed, Sergeant . . . I saw what looked like an undead feed. I mean there were parts . . . I mean bodies . . . it's something more though . . ." The warrior's voice drifted off into nothingness as his eyes glazed over and his ramblings died out.

The sergeant saw that he wasn't going to get any more out of the warrior so he stood and motioned the others to move out. The six warriors moved down the road. Three to each side as they closed on a small copse of trees in front of them.

As they got closer to the trees, the unmistakable stench of blood and a loud buzzing sound drifted on the morning breeze causing each warrior to tighten his hold on his weapon and sharpen his attention.

The group moved into the clearing and past the stopped armored vehicles and as one halted and looked in horror at the sight before them. A line of stakes was strung across the access road and on each was mounted the head of a Heoheska warrior.

As the unit stood in shocked silence, they watched flies and other insects crawling around and into the open mouths of their companions. A groan from the behind them shattered the warriors out of their stupor and they snapped around to see the only survivor of the massacre before them.

"It is time to quit acting like scared kittens and get a handle on this cluster . . ." the sergeant growled as another groan interrupted his command. "Cut him down and take the heads off those stakes," he said pointing to two warriors. "The rest of you spread out and keep an eye out for whoever did this. They may decide to come back for more fun." His men moved off to follow their leader's orders with grim determination.

The two warriors cut the sub-captain down and laid him out next to the armored vehicle while moving off to take care of the staked heads. The sergeant kneeled next to the sub-captain when the wounded warrior's eyes popped open and he grabbed the sergeant's arm pulling himself halfway up into a sitting position.

The sergeant startled then took ahold of the hand that had a death grip on his arm and pushed the warrior back down to the ground. "Whoa, Captain, settle down. You're safe now. Tell me what happened to your men?"

A low whisper came from the cracked lips of the sub-captain and the sergeant bent down closer to hear what he was trying to say. "What? What did you say, Captain?"

"Can't go . . . past . . . the . . . line . . . north . . . can't north . . ."

The sergeant leaned closer as the captain's words barely filtered through the sound of the flies buzzing around the clearing. He looked down as the captain's voice faded and saw that his chest was no longer rising and falling.

"Hey, Sergeant. What do we do with the heads?"

The sergeant looked down one last time at the dead sub-captain and then stood looking at the two warriors with the grisly pile in front of them. "Bury them with the captain here. And make it quick, we need to get back and let the commander know what the hell is going on . . ."

A low growl from the dead sub-captain drew everyone's eyes to his body as he quickly reached up and grabbed the sergeant's leg and sunk his teeth in. The sergeant's scream drowned out any more growls as the captain kept biting and worrying the warrior's leg like a dog with a new bone.

Fresh screams bounced around the clearing as the captain's teeth finally found flesh. Then the sound of a round hitting the captain's head echoed through the air as blood and bone splattered the sergeant. The unit ignored any danger from the surrounding area as they scrambled over to their leader.

"Sergeant, are you alright?"

"What the hell happened?"

"I thought the captain was dead."

The sergeant pulled his leg out of the truly dead grasp of the captain and growled, "Shut up and get back to your posts."

His voice shut down all conversation and all but two of his men moved back to their spots to keep watch. "Sergeant, I thought you said he was . . ."

"So, I was wrong before, Private." The three looked at the body then down at the bloody wound on the sergeant's leg. "Go on. Bury the heads and the body while I take care of this."

"But, Sergeant, I think . . ."

A low growl from deep within the sergeant's chest stopped the warrior from voicing his concerns and he and the other soldier walked off to start digging a grave. The sergeant grimaced as he ripped the leg of his uniform and looked at the teeth marks that were now bleeding freely. Yeah, when he got back him and that pissant lieutenant where going to have it out alright.

Chapter 7

We had been walking about an hour when we heard the echo of a weapon across the morning air. Stopping and crouching at the side of the road, I looked ahead to see if I could see any sign of Bo in the tall weeds. Turning my head, I was happy to see that Suzu had disappeared behind me. At least she had a good sense of self-preservation.

"That was a Heoheska weapon," Suzu's voice hissed from behind me.

"Quiet!"

Trying to stay as motionless as possible, I scanned the surrounding area when I heard Bo Jangles' voice ring in my head. *"It was about twenty miles south or so, Tanya."*

Taking a deep breath, I stood and looked down the road where I could see Bo prancing back to me. Turning, I looked back at where I thought Suzu was. "It's clear. Bo says the shot was toward the south part of town."

"I think you trust that 'thing' too much," the alien said as she walked over to me and watched the huge cat come up and sit down in front of us.

"Yeah, well, tell her I took her down, didn't I? Call me a thing, will she? Why I'll rip that overgrown piece of cat cra . . ."

"Bo play nice, she doesn't know you like I do," I said as I reached down and gave my best friend a rub between the ears before turning my attention back to the alien. "And as for you, stop insulting my friend. She has gotten me out of a few hairy situations before."

"What did it . . . I mean she say?"

"Just that she and you should be friends," I chuckled.

"GIRL, THAT IS NOT WHAT I SAID!"

"Yeah, I just bet that is what she said."

Laughing at the two of them, I took one last look around then nodded in the direction we were going. "Doesn't matter, we're heading north anyways. So, whatever is down south won't affect us." Suzu nodded as Bo just snorted and flipped her tail at the alien and moved off. As she disappeared into the weeds once more, I looked up at the bright morning light and then over at Suzu. "Come on, we're almost there."

"Where are we going?"

"You'll see once we get there. Just remember to be on your best behavior." Suzu looked puzzled then shrugged as we headed out after Bo.

An hour later the two of us were crouched behind a thin screen of trees as we looked out at the large building before us. Bo Jangles was moving around the outside of the building sniffing out the area to make sure we didn't run into any surprises. I started a little when I heard Bo's voice ring in my head. *"It's alright, Tanya. All I can smell is some orcs inside. I'll be there in a second."*

Grunting from the inactivity, I stood and heard a small pop from my knee and a chuckle. I shot a quick look behind me, frowning as Suzu popped up from the ground without a sound. "Bo said she will be here in a second and then we can go in."

"What is this place?"

Looking at the large blue sign with the yellow sun and white lettering on it, I laughed. "We're going shopping."

"Shopping?"

"Yeah, my dad . . . I was told that we needed to be prepared to move and I wanted to get us some supplies. Packs, sleeping bags, and stuff that I don't have back home."

"Why would we have to leave your home? Seems like you have been doing pretty good there from what I could see."

"Not my first choice, but it seems like your military is pushing north from Seattle. So, we need to be ready to go at a moment's notice."

"Oh."

"Yeah, oh. I have no intention of getting snapped up by them but if you want to stick around since they're your people you can."

The alien looked down on the ground then shook her head. "If you'll have me, I'll come with you. I really have no desire to go back. They . . . I mean . . ."

Suzu's voice faltered and I saw more tears streaming down her checks. "Listen, I'm sorry about your sister. I mean what you told me about what happened to her, but it might be better . . ."

The alien shook her head violently back and forth then she looked up at me and I could see that the tears in her eyes weren't sorrowful, they were angry. "It's not that, Tanya. They . . ." she stopped and looked down at the ground again.

I stepped closer to Suzu and laid a gentle hand on her shoulder. "They what, Suzu? What did they do to you?"

"The night I was taken . . . I was out by myself because I was trying to get away from my unit . . . they were trying to . . . to use me."

I stood there for a second trying to fathom such a thing when I did the only thing I could. I wrapped my arms around the alien before me and held her as the dam broke and she sobbed into my chest.

We stood like that for a few minutes until Bo's voice intruded on my mind. *"Uhm, I don't mean to break up this . . . well, whatever it is but we should get inside and find the things you need, don't you think?"*

"You're right, Bo," I said as I detached myself from Suzu and looked down at the cat staring up at us.

Suzu wiped the tears from her eyes as she followed my eyes down to the cat. "What is it right about?"

I laughed as Bo twirled away, flipping her tail at the alien. "She says we need to get going. That shopping is the best cure for what ails you. But first I need you to put this on," I said as I reached down and pulled a black watch cap out of my pocket.

"Why do I have to wear this?"

I sighed and pulled the cap out of her hands and put it on her pulling it down so that it covered the top part of her pointy feline ears. "There might be some orcs inside and I rather they think you're human than what you are. That is if you want us to get out of there in one piece."

"What the hell is an orc?"

I sighed again and looked back at Bo who was impatiently standing at the edge of the trees waiting for us. "Remember when I said that your bombs did more than kill humans?"

"They were not my . . ."

"Yes, yes, I know you didn't set them off. What I meant was . . . Never mind that. What I'm trying to tell you is that the stuff in the bombs had different effects on different humans. With me, it brought out magic as I told you before."

"Yes. And others?"

"Yeah, well, with others it changed them. It twisted their bodies and their minds. Mutated them so that they are what we call orcs. They are harmless, for the most part. They are cowards but they can be set off pretty easily when they think they are cornered or just plain don't like you. So that's why the hat."

"Okay, fine, I wear a hat."

Well, that was easier than I thought it would be. "Alrighty then. Just remember to be on your best behavior and keep cool."

Suzu looked puzzled then shrugged. "I'm not cold, but whatever you say."

I heard Bo's bark of laughter and watched the alien's eyes narrow as she looked at the cat. "What is so funny? It was laughing at me, wasn't it? That sound it made was laughter."

I held back my own laughter as I shook my head. "No, no, I think she had a hairball is all. She makes that sound when she has a hairball, Suzu."

Suzu nodded as she looked down at Bo. "Yes, that can be a problem at times."

"See, she understands. The alien understands how bad those are. So, I think you should show more compass . . ." Bo said as she strutted over to where we were standing.

Turning away from the alien and cat, I slapped my hand over my mouth and walked to the edge of the trees trying hard not to burst out laughing. From behind me, I could hear the alien mumble something about not seeing anything funny in hairballs while Bo's voice echoed the same sentiments in my head.

After a few minutes, I finally got my act together and could face the two of them without laughing. They stood side by side glaring at me. At least this was an improvement from them glaring at each other, I guess. "Come on you two let's go get our shopping done," I said as I turned and moved toward the store.

Glancing over my shoulder, I could see the two of them were following me to the double doors that stood open. Stopping at the opening, I waited for them to catch up to me. Bo brushed past me without another word and disappeared into the dark interior. Suzu stopped next to me and looked through the doors into the gloomy inside and then back at me. "We're going in there?"

"Yeah, it should have the biggest selection of the stuff we need. That is if the orcs haven't gotten to all of it." I unslung my crossbow from my back and made sure that it was cocked before stepping through the door.

"Heads up, girl. Three orcs in here and they are not in the best of moods."

Stopping, I whispered, "Bo said there are three orcs in here."

"Alright, now what?"

"Now we go shopping," I said heading to the sporting goods area.

Heoheska 3rd Scout Squad – South of Bellingham, WA.:

The dead or what was left of them were buried and most of his unit was resting while the sergeant and another warrior checked out the condition of the armored vehicles of the 'lost' unit. The sergeant stood outside while his driver bounced out of the second vehicle, a smile plastered on his face as he answered the unspoken question hanging in the air. "Both are okay as far as I can tell, Sergeant. We should be able to ride back to the command post instead of walking."

"No surprises that'll blow us up as soon as we start them?"

The warrior looked at the sergeant then back at each vehicle the smile disappearing from his face. "Well, Sergeant, I didn't see anything on either vehicle. I mean who could have set a trap on these? Those undead Earthers?"

"You think those undead from the cities killed this unit, Private?"

The warrior looked around the area and shrugged. "Sure, who else would . . ."

The sergeant slapped the warrior upside the head sending him back into the armored vehicle. "Private, you ever see the undead leave a body tied up or for that matter stake out a line of heads like we saw?"

"Well, no . . . I guess I haven't, Sergeant."

"Alright then, go over these vehicles again."

The private nodded and turned and crawled back into the armored vehicle. The sergeant twirled around and saw the rest of his unit sitting on the ground watching the exchange. "What the hell? You slackers have rested enough. I want you to make a thousand-meter sweep to make sure that we didn't miss anything."

All the warriors bounced to their feet and paired off and started to make their way out from the clearing. The sergeant growled as he watched his unit do their job when a wave of dizziness swept over him and his stomach roiled in protest. He leaned against the metal side of the vehicle until the sensation diminished. "Damn, must be getting old."

He stood there until the sensation departed and then turned to look at the freshly dug grave. He reached down and scratched his leg where the captain had bitten him as it started to burn and itch.

Chapter 8

Since I had been in this store numerous times, I knew exactly where we were headed. The two of us moved down the main aisle way, side by side, past the freezer section that had been without power for quite a while. "What is that smell?"

"I don't see how that could bother anyone who likes lima beans and ham, Suzu."

She gave me a puzzled look and shrugged. "What? It tastes good. Better than the food that we get from our cooks."

Laughing quietly, I shook my head at the thought of anything that could taste worse than lima beans and ham. "That smell is from the freezers. Once the power went out the food in them went bad. Or at least it went bad for me."

"You mean someone eats . . ."

Suzu stopped talking as we reached the last freezer section and the three orcs that were looting it figured out we were there. I looked at the three creatures. Two males and one female and shuddered a little, glad once again that my 'changes' weren't so apparent.

All three stopped filling the canvas bags they had in their hands, growls seeping through their warped mouths. I could see blackened, broken teeth gnash together as the three stared at us with hatred. There was no humanity left in those dark beady eyes.

Looking at the three, I thought I recognized their humped back twisted bodies and raised an open palm to them to try and reason with them. "We aren't here to take your food. We are here for our own stuff. Leave us alone and we'll leave you alone. Alright?"

The female of the group and the male closest to her stopped growling and started to look back into the freezer. Guess we caught these creatures on a good day I thought when the orc closest to us sniffed the air and his body went rigid. "Oh, damn," I whispered as I put myself between the three creatures and the alien.

"HESOHKAAAAA!" it slurred and yelled just as I heard Bo's voice ring in my head.

"TANYA, RUN! I screwed up. There is a whole pack of orcs in here not just those three."

As I heard the echoing yell coming from other parts of the store, I raised my crossbow and pulled the trigger. The bolt took the orc that yelled in the middle of the chest and slammed him into a pole in the aisle as I loaded the next bolt.

"HUMAN, DOWN!"

Looking up, I saw the other two orcs jumping at me and I got one more shot off taking the second male in the head. His dead body and the female hit me before I could reload taking all three of us to the ground in a tangled mess.

A loud curse and scream mixed and leaped from my mouth as I felt the teeth of the female bite into my left arm causing me to lose my grip on my crossbow. The pain doubled if that was possible as the female's mouth was ripped from my arm.

I caught a flash of silver and then saw a spurt of blood as Suzu swiped the knife I had given her across the orc's throat.

More yells echoed across the store as I felt a heavy weight land on my chest knocking the air out of me. *"Tanya,*

Tanya, please tell me you're not dead. Tanya say something." Trying to draw in some air the stink of cat food floated across my face as I groaned. Then the heavy weight on my chest disappeared as I heard Bo scream. *"PUT ME DOWN YOU OVERGROWN FLEA . . ."*

I saw Suzu toss Bo at my feet as she snarled, "She can't breathe with you on her, cat."

I finally caught my breath as I sat up cradling my wounded arm. I wasn't sure which I was happier to get rid of: the cat's weight off my chest or her stinky breath out of my face. *"Oh, right, sorry about that, Tanya."*

Nodding at the cat, I grit my teeth as the burning pain in my arm throbbed. Another set of yells sounding like they were only one or two aisles over echoed across the store and suddenly I was on my feet with the alien's arm wrapped around my waist. "Tanya, we need to get out of here now."

"My crossbow. Don't leave my crossbow," I whispered as the store started to go black.

Suzu felt the human go slack in her arms as she passed out. "Damn. We don't have time for this," she whispered as she shifted the girl and threw her over a shoulder then bent down and picked up the crossbow from the floor.

Turning, she started to run down the main aisle way when two of the orcs slid around the corner of the freezer and stopped in front of the alien. Before she could react a large ball of spitting mad fur flew past her head and slammed into the two orcs. *"Attack my friend, will you? You slimy little . . ."*

The cat's paw flashed out and Suzu saw the claws catch one of the orcs across the head to send it bouncing down the aisle way. Before the other orc could move, Bo grabbed it by the throat and gave a quick violent shake. There was a loud snapping sound as the orc went limp and the cat dropped the body in front of the alien. "Uhm, thanks, I guess. Now let's get out of here before any more of these things find us."

Bo turned and leaped over the headless orc body and headed for the front door as more orc yells echoed off the walls of the store. Suzu shifted the weight on her shoulder while drawing the knife and ran after the cat as she whispered to the unconscious human. "Guess your pet isn't as worthless as I thought."

The cat and alien broke out of the gloom of the store and into the bright sunlight of the day and as one turned toward the small grove of trees they had rested in earlier. Suzu could hear the voices of the orcs chasing them outside, but they seemed farther away than they had before.

Reaching the tree line, the alien carried Tanya a few more feet in before she eased the girl to the mossy ground. She watched the pale face for any flicker of movement as she whipped the crossbow off her back and cocked and loaded a bolt.

Her eyes were drawn back to the wide-open doors of the store as a group of six more orcs stumbled out into the sunlight. They stood there never getting far from the gloom inside as they surveyed the parking lot and the surrounding area.

A low growl beside her caused her eyes to shift to the large feline and then dart back toward the store as the creatures standing there finally gave up and stalked back inside. Suzu waited a few minutes before she bent down and checked the human lying next to her.

The girl's face was slack and red as sweat was beading around her forehead and lips. Suzu laid the back of her hand across the girl's head and pulled it back quickly as the heat poured off Tanya. "Damn."

Grabbing up the girl's arm she could see that the wound had stopped bleeding but had an angry reddish tint and a foul smell as green puss seeped from it. "Damn, damn. Not good."

Bo nosed her way under the alien's arm, let out a wretched meow, and looked up at the alien. Suzu opened a tiny bag that hung off her belt and shook her head as she rummaged through it finally pulling out a small silver vial. She looked down at the girl's arm that now had red streaks lacing out from the wound and then at the cat. "I'm not sure that this is going to work on humans. In fact, it could possibly kill her . . ."

"MEOWER!"

"Yeah, you're probably right if you said what I think you said. If I don't do anything she'll die anyway."

Bo Jangles watched as the alien uncapped the silver vial and poured the contents into her friend's wound. The smell of the poison running rampant inside her friend seemed to be coming from every pore of her body mixed with the sour smell of the young girl's sweat. Tanya moaned and thrashed for a few seconds before she calmed down again.

Both watched for a half hour as Tanya's color seemed to come back to normal. The fever went down while the wound stopped seeping that green puss. Bo sighed with relief as the smell of Tanya's sweat became less bitter and the scent of corruption slowly ebbed but didn't go away completely.

Suzu lifted the girl's head and poured some warm brackish water from Tanya's canteen past her cracked lips and down her throat. The girl choked most of it back up, but some did get into her. Capping the canteen, she glanced back at the doors of the store and then at the large cat that sat there watching her. "We need to get her back to the house in a hurry so that I can take better care of this wound."

Bo sat there for a second then she was off like a streak through the woods. The alien shook her head then slung the crossbow across one shoulder, bent down, and gently slung the young girl across the other.

"MEWORRRR!"

The cat's impatient voice sounded from the foliage in front of her and with a quick look back at the store, she shifted the girl's weight and started after Bo. "Yeah, yeah I'm coming, cat."

Heoheska 3rd Scout Squad – Advance Command Temporary Headquarters

The sergeant was standing with his sub-lieutenant next to him. Each stood at rigid attention before the commander and his command group. Neither of them made the slightest twitch or sound as their commander circled them in anger. Finally, the commander stopped behind the sub-lieutenant and growled. "So, Sergeant, I have your report that says that you and your men found this lost unit of ours and when you found them you came running back to tell us. Is this correct?"

"Sir, yes, sir, but we . . ."

The commander cut off the sergeant with his next question. "And you had no medic with your unit. Is that right, Sergeant? Is that why you let a sub-captain die out in the field and you had to treat your own wounds?"

The sergeant shifted his eyes to the side and saw the sub-lieutenant go pale as sweat started to bead on his forehead. "Sir, yes, sir."

It was quiet in the makeshift command post except for the shuffling of feet as the commander took a step back from the two men. The unmistakable sound of a pistol being cocked broke that silence as the commander whispered, "And where was the medic, Sergeant?"

The sergeant's eyes shifted again toward the sub-lieutenant and then snapped forward. "Sir, she was with the lieutenant, sir."

"Yes, that is where I thought she was." The sergeant didn't even flinch at the sound of the discharged weapon. The splatter of blood that whipped across his face. Or the sound of the sub-lieutenant's body hitting the ground.

The sound of the commander stepping up behind the sergeant was even louder than before as he whispered in the warrior's ear. "You do realize why I just did what I did don't you, warrior?"

"Sir, yes, sir."

"And that is, warrior?"

"Sir, that there is a time and place for . . ."

The commander gripped the back of the sergeant's neck and squeezed stopping the sergeant's answer. "Very good. Now get back to your unit. You are in charge of it until we can find a replacement for this . . ." The commander kicked the body lying on the ground while the sergeant turned, jaw clenched, and marched out of the command center. He made it about twenty feet behind the tent before he spewed his guts. The sweat ran off his forehead as he leaned against the side of his unit's armored vehicle.

A voice from the top of the vehicle whispered, "Sergeant, are you okay?"

The warrior straightened up wiping the sleeve of his uniform across his mouth as he growled, "Yeah, yeah, I'm fine. Wake up the rest of those slackers – I have news for them."

"Sergeant, they aren't feeling so well. I . . ."

The sergeant wiped his mouth once again trying to get rid of the vulgar taste as he growled up at the warrior, "I don't give a damn how they feel. Wake them up." The warrior disappeared inside the armored vehicle as worry creased the sergeant's brow. This was something more than getting old he thought as his mind wandered back to the sub-captain they had found just this morning.

Chapter 9

Bo moved through the trees never straying too far away from the alien and her precious cargo. The cat would stop every few minutes and sniff the air to make sure that they weren't followed by the orcs from the store. Or anything else that could be out and roaming now looking for an easy snack or two.

It had taken them the rest of the morning and most of the afternoon to cover the way back to the house since the alien had to stop and rest and check on her patient. Bo chaffed at the slowness but figured that they would make it back home before dark. She didn't even want to think what could happen if he caught them outside the house after dark with Tanya in her condition.

That's when the smell of corruption hit her nose. Bo stopped, turned, and sprinted back to where the alien had stopped.

Suzu was just putting Tanya down on the ground for a rest when the cat came running back and slid to a stop in front of her. She glanced over her shoulder then back at her. "MEOWRRR!"

The alien stood looking between the cat and the trees in front of her. "What? What is it? I don't see anything."

The cat hissed then glanced back over her shoulder. "MEOWWRRR!"

That was when the smell hit Suzu's nose too. The smell of undead Earthers. The smell she remembered so well from that day over a year ago as her unit was ripped to shreds by the undead. "Damn." She looked down at the young girl lying on the ground and then at the trees around her. She could now just start to make out the sounds of movement not far from where they stood. "Now what do we do? Any bright ideas?"

Bo nodded then leaped into the tree above them. Suzu looked up at the wide branches and the leaves that would give them cover and then shrugged. "Well, I guess it's better than anything I can come up with."

Suzu sighed then bent down and lifted the girl so that she could try and drape her over the lowest branch of the tree. She was surprised when the cat reached down and grabbed the girl's collar and started to help lift her up.

The two of them, working together, had themselves settled high enough in the tree so that anyone looking up wouldn't see them from below, hopefully. Suzu had just settled on a branch with the human cuddled in her arms when the first of the undead shuffled below the tree.

As she watched the movement below her, she counted twenty-five of the slow-moving undead move past them without even one looking up. She sighed in relief thinking it was a good thing that there hadn't been a breeze under the trees when Tanya moaned softly.

The alien sucked in a lung full of air as the movement below stopped and there rose a low moan from dead lips. "Oh, damn." As the undead surrounded the tree, she knew that she didn't have enough weapons to take care of all those bodies below. After a few minutes of listening to the moaning, she turned to where the cat had been sitting and found that she was gone. "Oh, great, that's it, abandon us when we need you . . . you damn flea-bitten . . ."

Bo watched as the zombies were drawn back to their tree like moths to an open flame. The undead gathered under them, their cold film-covered eyes full of their unnatural hunger glued to the meals sitting in the branches above them. Their moaning chorus got louder as their hunger-filled brains realized that they could not reach the food sitting just out of their reach.

The cat shifted looking for a way to get the alien and her best friend down out of the tree without becoming fast food when she caught a musky rank smell in the air. She smiled as she took one last quick peek at the human and alien before she leaped to the next tree.

The zombies below ignored the cat as she hopped from one tree to the next as their gaze was locked on the two larger bodies. Bo stayed in the trees moving from one to the other so that she wouldn't encounter any stray undead, following her nose as it lead her to the solution to their problem – if it didn't eat her first.

Bo stopped in an old apple tree that long ago gave up bearing fruit and looked down at the massive blackberry bush below her. One side of the bush slashed violently from side to side as loud grunts and growls issued from the large bear that was feasting on the late fall treat.

Bo leaped from the tree landing lightly on her feet and paused for a second as she eyed the massive black bear before her. As with most humans, the virus had affected the animals not in the initial blast zones. How it had affected this creature Bo saw clearly as its two heads reared up from devouring berries and sniffed the air.

As the creature ducked its heads and raked its giant paws at the berry bushes, Bo sighed. *Damn the things I must do for you, girl, to protect you. I hope this works* she thought as she streaked forward. Before she could chicken out, the cat swiped her claws against the thick rear hide of the bear before leaping back to the apple tree.

For a second nothing happened then the bear let out a huge roar with both its heads that shook the ground around the cat. *Well, that got his attention* she thought as the bear, with surprising speed for its bulk, whirled around to see what had interrupted its meal.

Both heads, beady little eyes blazing with anger, shifted from side to side until Bo's voice caught its attention. *"Hey, stupid, down here. What? You only got one brain between those two ugly heads."* Bo's voice rang inside the bear's head like a swarm of angry wasps.

The bear gawked at the cat in surprise not believing that any creature was stupid enough to attack something as big as it. *"What you do that for?"* Its voice reverberated through the cat's mind as though both heads had spoken the same thought at the same time.

Bo laughed. *"I did it because not only are you stupid you're ugly too and those are my blackberries you're in. So, move it, fatso, before I kick your butt."* Her laughter swirled in the bear's mind mixing with that angry buzzing and further enraging the animal.

It took the bear a few seconds to process Bo's words and the cat was afraid that her plan wouldn't work when it roared its anger and leaped toward the cat. Swiping one huge paw just above Bo's head, the bear splintered the old apple tree. Bo spun and sprinted back toward where her friends were treed as fast as her legs could carry her with the bear's hot breath singeing her tail fur. *"Oh damn, damn, damn . . . What the hell did I just do . . . damn . . . "*

Suzu loaded the last of her five bolts into the crossbow and carefully aimed down at the undead below her. She waited until two of the Earthers were lined up one in front of the other before she pulled the trigger. The bolt flew hitting the first undead creature in the forehead going all the way through and burying itself in the second head behind it. Both creatures stood for a second then dropped to the ground alongside four of their companions.

Unfortunately, that still left nineteen of the undead under the tree. Still too many to try an escape. What was even worse was that the human was starting to run a fever and there was that nasty smell coming from her wound again. Not as bad as before, but bad enough to kill her if she didn't get more medicine into her. Suddenly, a loud roar split the air and a streak leaped past the undead below and into the tree next to her.

Bo hit the tree halfway up and with two leaps was standing next to her human and the alien. *"Miss me?"* She laughed as she tried to catch her breath and another roar splintered the air. The bear came crashing through the foliage and right into the middle of the pack of zombies below the tree.

The zombies forgot all about the meal in the tree as the smell of flesh and blood crashed into their midst. The huge furry creature swiped one gigantic paw at the nearest body crushing its upper half against the tree. But before it could do any more damage the other zombies fell upon the bear to feast on their meal.

Suzu looked down as the bear fought for its life. It had its strength and weight behind it but in the end, the undead had the numbers. Though the creature did whittle those numbers down to two in the end before succumbing to the only outcome possible.

As the last two undead fed, Suzu glanced over at Bo and smiled. "Thanks. Guess she was right about you. You're not as dumb and useless as I thought you were." The smile disappeared as she looked down at Tanya. "We still need to get her home though and fast. I think the infection is kicking in again."

Bo blinked then hopped out of the tree taking one of the undead down to the ground. The unmistakable sound of crunching echoed through the woods as the weight of the cat smashed its head between it and the ground.

The other undead creature never looked up from its feeding as Suzu slipped from the tree and picked up a large branch from the ground. Walking up behind the creature, she set her feet and swung with all her might and a loud hollow crack echoed through the woods.

Suzu tossed the branch aside and looked down at the truly dead Earther before her. "That felt better than I thought it would."

Bo walked over to her and looked up with what Suzu could swear was a smile on her face. "MEOWRR."

"Yeah, me too, Bo. Thanks again for saving our skin."

"MEOWRRRR," the cat said as she rubbed against the alien's legs. A low moan from the branches brought the two back to their situation and both moved toward the tree and the young girl. They still had a way to go before any of them would be safe again.

Heoheska Command Center – South of Bellingham, WA

The 3rd scout armored vehicle was locked up tight as the major walked over and banged his hand on the side door. No sound came through the heavy armored side and once more the major pounded. "SERGEANT! SERGEANT, YOU AND YOUR MEN HAVE GUARD DUTY!"

No sound or movement from the vehicle. "What the hell? If these lazy . . ." suddenly the bolts of the door flipped open. "That's better, Sergeant . . ." The major opened the door of the vehicle and stopped talking as a low moan filtered from inside along with a putrid odor that assaulted his nose.

Hopping up on the bottom step, he looked into the murky recesses of the armored scout vehicle but his eyes couldn't penetrate the wall of darkness. "Sergeant? Sergeant, what the hell is that smell . . ."

Four hands reached out and grabbed the major and yanked him inside the vehicle before he could react. The armored doors slammed shut and no one heard his screams as the unit satisfied their hunger.

Ten feet away a darker shadow looked on with white shiny eyes and hissed. A hiss that was laughter as the vehicle rocked from side to side for a second before becoming still once more. "And so, it begins," he whispered as he turned and walked back into the night.

Chapter 10

Suzu shifted on the side of the bed and wiped a cool rag across the human's forehead and face, cleaning off the sweat and grime. Tanya thrashed and moaned a little as the coolness of the rag moved over her still too hot body.

The alien was worried. Ever since they had made it back to the house and she had given the human another dose of her medicine, she had expected the infection in the girl's arm to go down as it had with the first dose. As she watched the human though she could tell that all it was doing was keeping the poison from spreading but that wouldn't last long.

Bo hopped up on the end of the bed and sniffed at the girl then looked up at the alien with large pleading eyes. "Meowrrr?"

Suzu looked back at the cat and sighed. "I'm sorry. I'm doing what I can with what I have."

"MEOWRRR!"

"Yeah, well, same to you, cat. They never taught us about human meds and I don't want to put anything in her that would kill her and my meds don't seem to be helping . . ."

The scratching at the front door caused the alien to stop talking as she froze in fright. Bo leaped off the bed and scooted under it so that only her eyes were peeking out from the darkness. More scratching. Then a low hissing sound floated through the thick door.

Suzu stood up slowly pulling her knife from its sheath and glided over to the door. "Who's there?" Another whisper, a hiss leaked through the door causing the alien to lean her ear against it. "Who are you? What do you want?"

"My daughter . . . what have you done to . . . my child?"

Suzu took a step back from the menace that oozed through the door. She gulped down a lung full of air before answering. "I didn't do anything . . . it was the orcs . . ."

"If she dies . . . you will die." The hissing whisper was louder this time.

Suzu heard a hissing sound from under the bed and glanced at the cat. Her ears were laid back and her fur was all puffed out before she slunk deeper under the bed into the darkness.

The alien shook her head then turned back toward the door and pleaded, "Listen, my meds aren't working on her. She has an infection and I don't know your medicine well enough to treat her with it. Do you understand?"

"Yes."

Suzu waited for more, but the only sound in the room was the beating of her heart as it thundered in fright. "Are you still there? Can you help me?"

"Ye . . ." Before the voice could finish Suzu reached up and started to slide the door bolt open. She had moved it an only an inch then froze as a scream rent the night. "NOOOOOOOOOOOOOOOOOO!"

The click of the heavy bolt sliding back into place was loud in the night air. "I'm sorry. I thought you could help me. Help us."

"I will tell you what to give her. I . . . I can't be with her . . . with my daughter in her condition and so helpless. You will need the human first aid kit."

Suzu spun around and ran to the other room opening cupboards until she found a red kit and hurried back to the door. "I have one. It's a big re . . ."

"Yes, that is the one," the hissing whisper cut her off, "now look inside and find a round brown bottle marked 'Penicillin'."

She rummaged through the kit until she found several bottles like that. "I have it."

"Good. You must follow the instructions on the bottle, and make sure that she is given plenty of water. Do you understand?"

Suzu nodded then realized that whatever was on the other side of the door couldn't see her. "Yes, I'll do that."

There was silence on the other side of the door and she started to turn to start the new meds on the human when the whispered hiss stopped her. "Remember, Suzu, if she dies, you die. You too, cat . . . and I promise you that it will take you a very long time to die at my hands. A very long time indeed."

"I . . . I will do . . . I . . ." Suzu stopped talking then turned and walked over to the bed. She shook out two pills and forced them down the girl with a glass full of water. As she laid Tanya's head back down on the pillow, Bo crept out from her hiding place and hopped up on the end of the bed. "I take it that the big baddie daddy is gone?"

Bo didn't make a sound, she just circled at the bottom of the bed and curled up in a ball her eyes glued to the door. "Huh, guess not," Suzu whispered as her eyes followed the cat's gaze. She picked up the rag and wiped the sweat from the human's forehead and face.

Hours later, Bo still lay at the end of the bed and watched as the alien's head dropped to her chest and a light snore sounded in the room. The cat's head perked up when she heard a hiss from outside the door. "Yes, it is working. She will live."

The cat listened as the almost silent footsteps retreated and with as much caution as she could muster, she stood and slinked up the side of the bed toward Tanya's face. Quickly glancing around to make sure that the alien was still sleeping, she sniffed the shallow breath of the human girl and sighed with relief at the diminished stink of infection that had tainted her body. Slowly she sunk down next to the girl and laid her head across her chest where she could hear the stronger heartbeat and slept.

The sub-commander marched along the row of armored cars with his four warrior escorts. He was pissed that he was still up this late at night while he had a warm body back in his tent waiting for him. Reaching their destination, the escorts spread out around the vehicle as the senior officer pounded on the metal door. "SERGEANT! Sergeant, you and your men are to open this door now and come with me." He stood there fuming, determined that someone was going to pay for this inconvenience to him.

The commander waited, irritated that he now had to take care of a minor annoyance that he had sent his second in command to do a few hours ago. Where that officer had gotten to he had no idea, but as soon as he found him he would wish that he had never been born.

Standing back from the armored door, his patience at an end, he gestured to the nearest warrior. The soldier stepped up to the door and plugged a tiny electronic device into a side port and pushed a few buttons. A whisper-soft click sounded and the commander pushed the warrior aside, reaching up to grab the door handle.

The sub-commander was the lucky one. The heavy armored door burst open smashing him in the head and killing him instantly. The other four warriors didn't get a chance to die that easy. A nightmare leaped out from inside the vehicle and overwhelmed the escorts.

The seven starved undead Heoheska flew out of their armored crypt, the smell of fresh blood and living flesh caused a feeding frenzy. The screams of the eaten along with the howls of satisfaction from the undead bounced around the encampment alerting the command center and those nearby. Warriors rushed to the scene. Some to die under the unrelenting assault of the undead while others turned and ran. Still others, mostly those that had survived the first year on this hellish planet fought back and killed the undead.

After a long hour of fighting and dying, the last howls of the Heoheska zombies echoed off the surrounding hills. A lone dark figure stood within a small group of trees looking out, its white eyes blazing with the heat of its hatred. Glad that it had made it back from his daughter's home to watch the start of the killing. Now it was his turn. Slowly raising his arms, he whispered into the night wind. "Feed. Kill them all." From all around the encampment low moans rose.

The unit commander looked on as his warriors dispatched the wounded with a bullet to the head. At first, his men had balked at the task. Then as the wounded died, they began to rise again. There was no more hesitation, even those with a single bite or scratch were ruthlessly killed without another thought.

The unit's top sergeant materialized out of the dark and snapped a salute to his commander. "We have cleaned out the last of the undead and taken care of any warrior that could be affected, sir."

"Fine, Sergeant, fine. How many did we lose."

"One hundred men, sir."

As he stood there the realization washed over him that he had lost a third of his command from the six undead Heoheska warriors. A low moan riding the night breeze snapped his head around. He whipped his face back to his top enlisted man and barked, "I thought you said you got them all."

"We did, sir. I don't know . . ."

That's when the weapons' fire and screams started from the perimeter of the camp. Both warrior's faces went pale as a communication specialist came running up yelling at the two warriors. "SIR, WE'RE BEING HIT FROM ALL SIDES BY EARTHER UNDEAD."

The top non-com and officer stood frozen in place as the warrior, face fixed in fright, looked between the two of them waiting for either to give an order. "Sir . . . we . . ."

The commander grabbed the warrior's arm and spun him around toward the nearest armored car. "In there. Both of you, we need to . . . we need to get . . ."

The sergeant grabbed the commander's arms, snarling, "We can't leave the men . . ."

The commander, without a word, pulled his sidearm and shot the sergeant in the face. As the body fell, he grabbed the warrior in front of him and pushed him toward the vehicle that sat on the edge of the encampment dropping his weapon from nerveless fingers. Once they reached the open door, he pushed the protesting warrior into the car and slammed the heavy metal door shut hitting the lock button before the putrid smell of the dead reached his nose.

The undead unit sergeant was crouched in the corner of the vehicle. Some small sense of self-preservation made him crawl into the lone armored car as others of his kind had died in the night. Now food had crawled within the armored tomb and he didn't fight the hunger that surged through his mind pushing him with its burning need to feed.

The dark figure watched as the armored car rocked back and forth for a few minutes as the last of his enemies died. As his zombie army fed, his eyes blazed with satisfaction. He smiled and walked off into the early morning light.

Chapter 11

As I fought the darkness I tried to breathe but it felt like my chest was being pushed by a heavyweight when I heard a voice snarl, "Get off her, cat. I told you before that you're too heavy to lay on her." And the weight disappeared.

There was a loud thump on the floor and a hiss sounded nearby. I didn't care, I could catch my breath again. Lying there, I listened to the sounds around me and tried to concentrate on my friend now that I could get some air again. *"I was trying to keep her warm, you flea bagged . . ."*

"Bo?" The voice in my head stopped complaining and I heard a gasp from beside me. Slowly, I opened my eyes and looked up into the worried face of the alien as I felt the cat jump up on the end of my bed. "Where are . . ."

"Hush, human. We are back in your home."

"How? What?"

"An orc bit you, girl. Good thing you had this oversized kitty with us or you would have died . . ."

"You're fine. You were poisoned by an orc and we got you back here . . ."

Listening to the two try to tell me what happened just made my head hurt more than it already did and I held up a weak hand to stop them. "Please, just one at a time."

The two of them stared at each other, then the furball at my feet sighed and nodded at the alien. *"Fiiiiine, I am tired*

82

anyway. Let the overgrown kitty tell you how she saved your life," Bo said as she sniffed and then turned her back to us while flicking her tail and laying her ears back.

Suzu chuckled at the cat's attitude then turned back to me with a tired smile. "Do you remember being in the store and being attacked by the orcs?"

"It's fuzzy, but, yeah, I think one of the little . . . anyways, I think I got bit. Did I get bit?"

"Oh, you got bit alright and whatever kind of poison they have in their mouths went right to work on you."

"Guess they don't floss every day." The alien gave me a puzzled look. "Don't worry about it, just trying to make a joke. What happened then? I don't remember anything."

"The short version is that I got you back here with a lot of help from your cat and we got the proper meds into you."

At the mention of Bo's help, I noticed that her tail stopped flicking back and forth and her ears came up from the top of her head slightly. I looked back at Suzu and smiled as she shook her head at the cat's antics. "How did you know what meds to use?"

"I tried some from my med kit first and that seemed to help a bit, but you were still sick and I wasn't sure what to give you until . . ."

As she talked to me, I could see Suzu go a little pale. "Until what?"

"He stopped by, Tanya, and told 'Hello Kitty' here what medicine to give you."

I could see where a visit from my daddy would scare even an Heoheska warrior. "Bo said that my Daddy came by and let you know what to give me."

Her eyes flickered to the cat then back to me as she nodded and then shuddered. "Yes, he did. He, sort of, let me know that if you died I and the cat here would be sorry in most unpleasant ways."

"Sorry about that. Even when he was human, he was slightly overprotective of me."

Bo snorted. *"Slightly?"*

"Enough, Bo," I said as I shifted one foot and rubbed against the side of the furball lying between my legs.

"Fine. Fine. But ask the alien kitty there about our other problem."

Trying to sit up, I looked over at Suzu. "Problem? What problem? What's Bo talking about?"

The alien looked daggers at Bo who flicked her tail and ignored her before turning back to me. Just before dawn, I opened the windows to give you some fresh air . . ."

Shooting up in bed, I had forgotten that I still wasn't feeling that good when a wave of dizziness reminded me of that fact. "YOU DID WHAT!" I yelled and then slowly sunk back on the pillow as my head pounded.

"Don't worry about it. Bo was good enough to check the perimeter of the house so I figured it was safe. Besides, you needed the fresh air and we needed to get rid of the stink of infection in here."

"Alright, fine. So, what was the problem then?"

Suzu didn't say a word for a second as she looked down at me then sighed. "We . . . I mean Bo and I heard weapons fire early in the morning. It was pretty far away and faint, but . . ."

I nodded. "But you could hear it nevertheless. Could you tell whose?"

"It wasn't Earther's, Tanya. There isn't anyone else around that would have weapons. It was my people."

I shook my head then thought of a small rumor I had heard about two months ago and smiled. Suzu gazed at me, puzzled. Bo must have read my mind because she snorted. *"Don't get your hopes up, girl. You know that that traveler was three quarters the other side of crazy when he came through here. I told you then that you couldn't believe him."*

I sighed then snuggled back into my pillow. "Yeah, you're right, Bo. He was as crazy as a bed bug. Wasn't he?"

"Crazier, girl. Crazier."

Suzu's head swiveled back and forth between the two of us until she let out an exasperated sigh. "I really hate that when you two do that. It's frustrating to listen to one side of a conversation. What are you two talking about now?"

"About two months ago or so we had a crazy man come through. He said that there was a group of humans that hadn't been changed . . . you know like the orcs. That they had a fortress up in the mountains and were planning on taking back our world."

"And you stayed here?"

"Like I said, he was a looney. He said a lot of things that were crazy. I gave him some food and sent him away."

"You never saw him again?"

"It wasn't your fault, Tanya. The man was so crazy there was no telling what he would have done."

I looked down at my friend and shook my head at the words that quietly filtered through my mind. "I should have done more, Bo."

Looking puzzled again and more than a little annoyed Suzu's eyes took in the two of us. "What is it?"

Sighing, I whispered. "We found him two days later. Or rather what was left of him . . ."

"The undead?"

I shook my head. "No, my daddy. The next night he came to visit me and told me that I was to stay here and to not help anyone else that came around. That he was only trying to protect me."

"Yeah, I sort of got that attitude from him last night."

"Sorry about that," I apologized again. Suzu nodded then we sat quietly as a light morning breeze filtered through the open window and lightly brushed its way across my body making me shiver.

Suzu pulled up the blanket around my legs displacing Bo for a second. She tucked it around me then as the cat settled back down. I could feel my eyelids start to droop. "Why don't you get some more sleep? I'll wake you in two hours and we'll get some more of these meds down you."

"Yeah, thanks. I guess I'm still not a hundred percent yet, am I?"

The alien nodded, but a small smile played at the corner of her lips. "You're pretty tough for a human, but yeah, you're not there yet. Give it a day or two and we'll have you up and about though, okay?"

Nodding as sleep started to overtake me, I opened my eyes slightly as a thought flashed into my head. "Suzu, you won't leave me, will you? I mean you will be here when I wake up, right?"

She laid a hand on the side of my face and caressed my cheek. "I promise that I will never leave you, okay?" Nodding once more, my eyes closed and I finally let myself drift off.

Suzu sat watching the human's breathing even out into sleep and then glanced down at the cat that gazed back at her and whispered so as though not to disturb her patient. "As soon as she is able, we are going to have to get out of here. Whatever happened down south won't keep them from coming up here for long."

The cat glanced out the window then back at the alien and nodded her understanding. Suzu nodded then leaned back in her chair and tried to think of all the things they would need to survive in this world away from this small fortress.

She started to get up thinking of doing a quick inventory while Tanya slept, but sat back down when the girl moaned in her sleep. Inventory could wait for a few hours she thought as she closed her tired eyes and drifted off.

A half hour later her head hit her chest and then popped up as her stomach growled. She opened her eyes and looked at her watch seeing that she had been out for a while as her stomach let out another growl. She watched the girl peacefully sleep for a few minutes before she slid out of her seat and headed to the kitchen.

There was a few of those brown meal packages on the counter and grabbing one she opened it and pulled out the first big green pouch. Opening it with her knife, she dug out some of the food and gulped it down.

She got half of it down when she felt her stomach do a little flip. She put the bit of food that she was holding in her hand back in the bag. "Damn, that is not lima beans and ham."

"Meowrrr?"

Suzu looked down at the cat and then at the bag she held. "What? You want this crap?"

"Meowrrr!"

"Yeah, no problem. You can have it," she said as she poured the contents of the green bag on to the floor. Bo pounced on the pile and dug into the mess with some gusto. "I always knew you were stupid if you like that garbage, animal."

Bo never looked up from her feast as she finished her meal. From the other room Suzu could hear the young girl moan and thrash around so giving the cat one last disgusted look she returned to sit by her patient.

A lone single-seat scout glider moved across the old highway. Its powerful but small quiet engine kept the machine skimming only a foot above the old roadway as its pilot kept his eyes roaming from side to side watching the woods.

The glider was long thin and mostly engine – built to get a scout out of trouble fast. Which was good since it had no weapons except what its pilots carried. This scout had been traveling since early morning looking for the northern advance unit that had sent out a distress signal just before dawn.

As his head swiveled from side to side, he could feel the rumble of the gilder under him as it strained and pulsed at the slow speed that he kept his machine at. He knew that the gliders were meant to run at max. A quick get in and get out option, but as usual, the high command had their own way of doing things.

His mind processed the area around him as another part of him grumbled about the mission at hand. This should have been a job for the foot scouts or an armored scout unit, but no it was up to him to take his priceless machine and come . . . He slid his glider to a stop, his eyes wide behind his goggles as he took in the sight before him.

Across the road, a line of Heoheska skulls were all staring back at him. The birds and insects that had scattered at his gilder's approach settled back down to resume their feeding on what flesh dangled from the grisly sight before him.

The scout's hand moved down toward his weapon, thoughts of killing some of the birds flashing through his mind. Then he stopped, it wouldn't matter now to the dead warriors before him and could bring Earther undead down on him. With a quick glance around he turned his glider and, without a backward glance, sped back down the highway.

Chapter 12

Suzu woke the groggy human up a few hours later and forced another couple of pills and some water down her before Tanya dozed off again. After her last nap, the alien was restless and since the sick young girl seemed to be sleeping soundly, she decided she would get a quick inventory started.

As quietly as she could, she got up from her chair and stretched as Bo eyed her with suspicion. "What? I'm just going to look around some," she whispered as the cat laid its ears back and flicked its tail at her.

"MEOWRRR."

"Quiet, I'm not leaving. Okay?" she whispered.

The cat gazed at her for a second then huffed as she laid her head down. Suzu took that as an okay and wandered into the kitchen where she started to quietly open and close doors checking what was in each cabinet.

Most of the space around her was filled with those brown plastic bags that held food. She looked at the black writing on the packages wishing that she could read Earther better when she let out a fishy-tasting burp from her previous meal. She waved her hand as her nose wrinkled at the smell. "That wasn't as good as those green and brown meals Tanya gave me, but at least I won't starve anytime soon." Another burp erupted and she teared at the nauseous cloud that hung in the air.

"Meowrrr?"

Suzu spun around looking down at the cat at her feet and growled, "Damn, don't sneak up on me like that, beast."

"Meowrrr?"

"What? I don't understand you. What do you want? I'm not opening another one of those bags until Tanya wakes up and can tell me which one is the good stuff."

The cat wound around the alien's legs then marched over to a double set of doors that stood at the other end of the kitchen. Suzu sighed and followed the cat over and stood before the doors. "MEOWRRR!" the cat howled as she nudged the closed doors.

"Quiet! I'll open the damn doors, but if you wake the human I am going to skin you alive, cat." She reached up as the cat sat back and watched her attentively, her tail flipping back and forth, her eyes wide.

Behind the doors was a tiny closet that held shelves loaded from top to bottom with an assortment of cans and bags that all had different pictures of cats on them. Before she could say anything, Bo Jangles crouched then leaped past the alien landing on the top shelf. "What the hell are you after now, cat?"

"Meowrrr!"

The cat rummaged all the way behind the bags on the shelf, her tail waving back and forth as her loud purrs echoed in the kitchen. Then the tail and purring stopped and Bo scrambled backward dragging a couple of small bags in her mouth. "What is that, cat?"

Bo crowed in triumph as she found the bags she was looking for. A tiny bit of guilt fleetingly tainted her mind, but it fled as she thought of the substance that was in each of these bags. She dragged them to the edge of the shelf and dropped them into the waiting hands of the alien.

Suzu stood looking down at the two bags then back up at the cat. *"Well, don't just stand there. Open them up you overgrown kitty,"* Bo said as she hopped down from her perch and looked up expectantly at the alien.

Suzu stared at the bags and then down at the cat whose tail was once again whipping from side to side as her purr started buzzing as loud as an armored scout car engine. The alien glanced at the cat, shook her head in puzzlement then raised the bags to her nose and took a quick sniff.

Suddenly, the strange smell that seeped from the edges of the bag hit the inside of her nose and she felt lightheaded and blood rushed to her face for a second. "Oh, damn," she whispered as she ripped open the two bags and brought both up to her nose and took a deeper snort of the contents.

Bo looked up at the alien as she inhaled the smell of the catnip and snarled as she sunk her claws into the alien's leg. *"HEY, I FOUND THE STASH. GIVE ME SOME!"*

Suzu pulled her nose out of the bags glaring down at the cat before she threw one of them across the room. Bo leaped in the air spinning around and chasing the bag grabbing it between her front paws before it hit the ground. The cat and the bag hit the floor skidding forward until they struck the kitchen counter where the cat flipped over purring as the contents spilled all over her.

Suzu watched the cat's antics for a second before she leaned against the wall and closed her eyes as she brought the bag up to her nose and took a large sniff of the stuff inside. Slowly she slid down the wall, a large vacant smile crossing her face.

"Ooooh, look I can smell the colors." The smooth low tone of Bo Jangle's voice made me jerk up in bed causing a wave of dizziness to wash over me. As the room spun for a few seconds, I held my head in my hands and groaned.

A loud titter of a laugh made me raise my head and I looked back toward the kitchen when I heard Bo again. *"Can you smell them you overgrown kitty?"* I heard more laughter. One that high titter and the other a low purring laugh from my cat.

Shaking my head, I gingerly swung my legs to the side of the bed. Trying to decide if I really wanted to know what was happening in the kitchen, I glanced out the open window and saw that it was starting to get dark out. "Suzu? Bo? Why is the house still open?"

Bo's slurred voice echoed in my head. *"Oh, are we afraid that daddy-waddy will come and see us Tanya-Wanya?"*

Groaning, I got up from the bed. I didn't have any more dizziness, which was a good thing. Shuffling over to the windows, I closed and locked them as more laughter echoed from the kitchen. "I am so going to kill you, Bo," I whispered as I checked that the door was locked too.

Taking a deep breath, I counted to ten before heading toward the kitchen. I stopped at the door and took another breath thinking of all the nasty thing I was going to do to that damn cat when I realized that the two in there were no longer laughing.

Turning the corner into the room, I stopped and stared at the sight before me. There were MRE and opened cat food cans spread all over the floor with the alien and Bo lying in the middle of all that mess tangled in a heap. "What the hell?" I whispered as I took a step forward and my foot kicked a bright blue bag across the floor.

"Ooooohhhh, don't yell so loud, Tanya," Bo moaned as she rolled off Suzu's stomach and hit the floor with a loud thump.

That brought a low moan from the alien as her head wavered back and forth. "Oh, please someone put me out of my misery if you all are going to yell so loud."

Giggling, I stomped over to the two which elicited more moans from them. "Serves you right. Getting into the catnip like that. Bo, you know what that stuff does to you, and I don't need you getting Suzu hooked on that crap either."

Reaching down, I helped the alien up off the floor. She didn't protest too much even though she did sway from side to side as I got her feet under her. "I don't feel so good, human."

"Oh, don't . . ." but it was too late as she bent over and emptied the contents of her stomach all over the floor. "Oh, damn, let's get you to bed," I said as I maneuvered her around the mess and into the other room.

Getting her laid out on the bed, I got a wet cloth and wiped down her face. "Come on. How about we get you changed . . ." the soft snore caught me mid-sentence and I shrugged as I got up from the bed and headed back to the kitchen. Guess clean up would wait till she woke up.

Holding my breath, I stomped over to Bo and grabbed her up from the floor holding her up to my face where she abruptly let out a loud belch then started snoring. Taking shallow breaths, I stalked to the kitchen door and tossed the cat across the room where she bounced on my bed and lay still as though dead to the world. With the mood I was in she was lucky she had passed out or I might have been tempted to kill her.

Sighing, I turned and looked at the mess in the kitchen and leaned back against the wall for a second. The good news was that I seemed to be feeling better. The bad news was since I was the only one feeling better I was elected to clean up this mess.

Standing up from the wall, I went to collect some cleaning supplies when I heard two loud burps and groans from the other room. Laughing loudly brought more sleepy groans of pain from the other room.

It was almost nighttime before the armored column started up from the northern edge of Seattle. The heavy armored units were being kept around the larger cities to take care of the large number of Earther dead that never seem to diminish even after months of destroying them.

Three trucks lead the way. Their turrets slaving left and right looking around for some target to kill with their weapons. Behind them, two main battle tanks followed with four troop and supply carriers tagging behind. One last truck brought up the rear guard. Its turret turned to the rear as it watched the back of the column for any attack from that direction.

The heavy firepower of this unit headed due north. All the warriors in this unit were now veterans of fighting the Earther undead and no one doubted in the least that they would be able to destroy whatever had decimated the scout units to the north.

Watchful bright white eyes watched the unit move north. The dark figure brought a tethered hawk to its face and hissed a few words into its ears. With a quick jerk, the tether was released and the hawk flew low over the tree line as it too headed north.

Chapter 13

I guess I shouldn't have taken so much enjoyment in banging around the bucket and mop as I did, but each groan and moan, from the other room, did make the cleaning a little easier and more enjoyable. By the time I was done, the kitchen was scrubbed cleaner than it had been in a long time and there was one large trash bag stuffed full waiting to be burned.

"Ooohhhh, what did I do?" Echoed in my head as I heard a large thump from the other room.

I peeked in and saw Bo lying on the floor looking raggedy. Her fur stood out in all directions and her ears were flat against her head. "You awake, Bo? Want some yummy cat food. Maybe some liver and fish chunks."

I saw her heave for a second then she dashed for the small door that led outside. *"Ooohhh, Tanya, don't . . ."*

Laughing, I shook my head at her retreating back. "Serves you right, cat. That is the last time we have catnip around here."

"Oh, I'll never again . . . rhurgggg . . . oooohhhh . . . rhurgggg . . . oh, I promise . . . rhurgggg . . ."

I tuned out the cat's heaving as I laughed some more at her discomfort. "Yeah, that's what you said last time, Bo."

A low groan came from the other bed and then a whisper that I could barely make out. "What did that cat give me? Oh, gods, it feels like my head is stuffed full of dirt and my stomach like it has something squirming in it."

Stomping over to the bed, I smiled down at the alien as she held her head in her hands and moaned. "So, I take it you don't have catnip on your planet?" I smirked.

Suzu's eyes were opened mere slits as she gave a tiny shake of her head. "That stuff is so evil. No, we don't have anything like that on our planet. What is it? I felt so good at first then . . ." she went pale as she swallowed and then slammed her mouth shut so hard I could hear her teeth click.

I laughed some more at the poor alien then sat on the side of her bed which elicited another loud moan from her as she rolled over and dry heaved. I stopped laughing as I watched her heave once more. "You make a mess again, you clean it up."

"Again?"

"Yeah, you and that damn cat trashed the kitchen and I got stuck cleaning it up since neither of you were in any shape to do it."

"Sorry."

"Sure, sure, just don't make another mess. Okay?"

"Alright . . ."

The scratching noise at the door quieted both of us. Even the faint voice of Bo Jangles in my head went quiet. The two of us stared at the door when another louder scratching sounded and a voice hissed, "Daughter, I know that you are awake. I have information for you. You must listen to me. Daughter, do you hear me?"

Easing myself off the bed, I slunk over to the door and leaned against it. "I'm here, Daddy. What do you want to tell me?"

"You are feeling better. I don't smell any more infection on you, Daughter."

"Yes. I'm fine," I glanced behind me and softly chuckled at the green face of the Heoheska warrior. "We're all fine, Daddy. What is wrong?"

It was quiet for so long that I thought that my father had left when I heard a hissing that I knew from experience was his laughter. I felt a little sad remembering the raucous laughter that was once my dad's trademark. "I smell that Bo has introduced your friend to the delights and danger of catnip."

Not being able to do anything but laugh along with him, I glanced back at Suzu and watched as her face turned a deep red. "Yes, but what is so important you had to come and warn us?"

It was quiet again the laughter dead when I heard a deep intake of breath and that hissing again. "The aliens have sent a heavy armored unit up here to find the ones that have been giving them trouble. You need to get what things you can together and leave tomorrow morning or I should say this morning. I am not sure that we can keep them back for long."

"Where can we go, Daddy? There isn't any place where we can hide from them, is there?"

"You need to head out to Mount Baker, Daughter."

I waited for more, then when nothing else came I asked. "Why there?"

"There are humans there. Humans that are not like the orcs or me . . ."

"How is that possible?"

There was that hissing laugh again. "It seems that I wasn't the only paranoid in the country. There is a small base built in the mountain by a group that had the money to throw around. Rich men that believed that our country was going downhill fast and wanted to be prepared for it."

"So, these guys survived?"

"No." Another hissing laugh. "They died like all the rest, caught out of their fortress all that is but their men. Men that were hired to defend the rich were saved in the base. They are there now with their families."

"So that crazy man wasn't so crazy after all."

"No, no, he wasn't, but he shouldn't have gone around babbling about the base either."

"Is that why you killed him, Daddy?" It was quiet. No hissing. No laughter. "Daddy? Daddy, are you there?"

"What are we going to do, Tanya?"

Turning, I gazed into the wide alien eyes of Suzu and shrugged. "I guess we leave in the morning. Get some sleep. You need to be in good shape before we head out tomorrow."

"What are you going to do?"

I smiled and shrugged again. "I'm going to do what I need to do. Pack what we have and figure out what we need, and where we can pick it up from."

"But the orcs?"

Don't worry about them, Suzu. When we go back we are going in with some firepower. I only use the crossbow because it's quiet and I didn't want to draw any attention to us. I guess that doesn't matter anymore, does it?"

Suzu laid back on the bed and closed her eyes as I opened my mind to Bo Jangles once more. "Bo, did you catch that? We leave in a couple of hours. Get some sleep." I heard a gentle snort in my head then a snore. Okay then, I thought, as I walked over to a closet and started to dig out two older army surplus backpacks from deep within it.

The armored vehicles moved slowly through the night. The first three trucks were grinding ahead in a triangle formation with the carriers in a square formation behind them flanked on each side by the heavy tanks. The last truck was spaced behind the group watching for any vehicles that broke down or strayed from the formation.

The heavy vehicles passed over the road and the surrounding ground without rolling over the tiny open holes in the ground. All, that is, except the last armored truck. The front end moved over the hole activating a tiny sensor in the end of the weapon. When the middle of the truck rolled over the hole, a small rocket lit up and shot a molten spear straight up. Unfortunately for the Heoheska, they had never run into a landmine before.

The superheated metal flew up and on contact with the thinner bottom of the truck, it punched through spreading the shrapnel up and outward tearing into flesh, fuel lines, and ammo. The armored truck rolled forward a few more feet then exploded from the inside out in a fireball that tore apart the dark night.

The other vehicles ground to a halt, their weapons spinning looking for an enemy to unleash them on. After a few more minutes of no other action, the lead vehicle started moving forward with the others following close behind leaving the funeral pyre burning behind them. In other holes around the road, other mines waited to be activated.

Dark watchful human eyes looked down on the scene below as a voice whispered from the watcher's right. "Damn, Captain, I thought for sure we would get more than one."

The small camouflaged soldier turned briefly smiling at the bigger body lying next to him. His even white teeth the only thing showing in the dark painted face. "Don't sweat it, Sarge. There will be more of them coming this way and then we'll bar-be-que more aliens."

Both soldiers chuckled as the wind carried the smell of cooked flesh up to their hiding place. Two others wearing the same uniforms crawled over from their observation point cutting short the humor of the two senior soldiers. "From where we were, Captain, it looks like no one got out."

The captain stood and stretched as the last sounds of the armored vehicles faded in the night. He looked down at the burning vehicle then at the three soldiers standing awaiting new orders. "Okay, I want you two to wait till the fire dies down some then plant two more of these little babies. One on each side of that vehicle. Oh, and put a few surprises around the back of the vehicle too."

All four grinned knowing that any following vehicles would go around the armored tomb trying to avoid running into the same fate. The other surprises were for the Heoheska recovery crew that would probably come out and salvage what they could from the armored truck.

"Yes, sir. We'll take care of it right away."

Both senior soldiers nodded then turned to walk back to one of the hidden vehicles set in a small grove of trees at the bottom of their hill. The captain turned and looked down one last time at the truck whose fire was just now starting to die down. "Oh, and boys . . ."

"Yes, sir!" Both privates snapped to attention and looked at the captain expectantly.

The captain smiled at his men. "Get the job done fast and try like hell not to get eaten by the zombies, hear me?"

Both soldiers smiled back as they echoed each other. "YES, SIR!"

The two senior soldiers turned and moved quietly down the hill, their eyes alert for any sign of the zombies that they had warned the others of.

Chapter 14

"Tanya. Tanya, wake up.

Opening my eyes to just a slit, I looked down at the cat on my lap, her face only inches from mine. "Oh god, your breath stinks, Bo," I said as I sat up straighter knocking the 'fluffy' cat off my lap.

"Yeah, well, girl, your breath doesn't smell like summer flowers either."

Rubbing my eyes, I laughed as Bo flicked her tail at me and stalked off in a huff toward the other room. I was glad to see that she had recovered from her little bender. I would need her at her best if we were going to start off for that base in the mountains this morning.

Sitting there dreading leaving the only home I had ever known, I looked around and sighed before getting up and grabbing breakfast for the three of us. After opening Bo's food, I marched into the other room chirping with my best early morning sweet voice as I threw an MRE in the general direction of Suzu's bed. "Come on, sleepy head. Up and at 'em." I laughed at the smack and groan from the bed. Damn, I wasn't such a bad shot after all.

"What time is it?"

"It's time to get lazy butts out of bed and get moving unless you want to be here waiting for the company to arrive."

Suzu sat up fast at that and looked around confused for a second. "So last night wasn't a dream?"

I couldn't help but laugh as I heard a tiny chuckle from Bo Jangles ring in my head. "No, it wasn't a dream. My father told us we need to leave today and, yes, there is somewhere we can go. Hopefully, there is somewhere that is," I said as my laughter trailed off.

The alien sat up and nodded as she opened the MRE I had tossed her and started to dig into the main meal pouch. "So, what do we need to pack?"

"Already taken care of." She stopped eating and looked over at the two packs leaning against the door.

"I see you've been busy. How are you feeling?"

I gave her my best smile. "I'm fine. I won't be running any marathons, but, hey, I can hack a little hike in the woods."

"Okay then, I guess after breakfast?"

"Sure, no time better," I said as I opened my own MRE and started in on breakfast.

After a quiet hour of eating and each of us drifting off into our own thoughts, I jerked around at the large belch that came from my bed. "Bo! Really?"

"Sorry, you two are just such dull company this morning. Thought I needed to liven this party up a bit."

I shook my head at my cat then threw the MRE bag to the floor. "Guess it's that time then."

Suzu looked down at her clothes with a grimace then back up at me. "Do we have time for me to get a little cleaned up and changed?"

Nodding, I pointed at the kitchen. "Yeah, I have some clothes laid out and there is some water in the basin for you to wash up with. I need to get some stuff out of the weapons' locker anyways. Just don't take long."

Suzu hopped off the bed and almost ran into the kitchen while I reached under my pillow and pulled my rag doll out from under it. Walking over to my pack, I stuffed her into a tiny side pocket making sure that it was secured before I knelt by the side of Suzu's bed and pushed a button set into the floor.

A small door slid to the side and I heaved a heavy box out of the hole it had been hiding. Sliding it across the floor, I went back and dug out another box. Then made two more trips before Suzu was done cleaning up and changed into cleaner clothes. "What are these?"

I smiled up at the alien while bending down opening one of the bigger boxes. "These babies are a present from my daddy."

Suzu moved so that she was standing looking down into the lined box. "I've never seen anything like those before, but they look wicked."

Reaching down I picked up the weapon and slung the strap across one shoulder so that it lay across my back and chest. The alien's eyes went wide as she looked at the miniature multi-barreled weapon. "This was the latest prototype in miniguns that a friend of my daddy was working on before you guys came along. In fact, the only two in the world are here in these boxes. He nicknamed them Wasps."

"How did your father get them?"

"Seems that the government found out about them. Soooo my daddy's friend decided to hide them before they were taken from him. That was right before the bombs went off and he never did come back for them. So, I guess they're mine now."

"How do they work?"

I kicked one of the smaller boxes over to Suzu. "Open that and hand me one of those magazines."

Suzu eagerly bent down, flipped the box open, and whispered as she picked up one of twenty magazines that the box held and then handed it to me. "You take this and slap it in the opening on top here." I slammed the magazines down with the palm of my hand. "Make sure it's seated then pull the trigger here on the back handle while holding the front handle with your other hand."

"Oh!"

"Yeah, that about says it all. My daddy took one of these babies out before the day and showed me what they could do. Let's just say if you shoot at a zombie with one of these there is no need to aim for the head. Oh, and don't hold down the trigger or you will zip through your ammo in a few seconds."

"Then how . . ."

"Just pull the trigger and release. Believe me, it will be enough." I hit the release on the side by the magazine and it popped up. Taking the strap off, I took the weapon off and walked over to a small door set in the wall. Hitting a hidden switch along the molding below it the door popped open. Reaching in I grabbed two belts and holsters, tossing one in Suzu's direction. "For close personal protection."

The alien pulled the pistol out of the holster and looked at it for a second before she raised one eyebrow. I strapped my belt on and pulled the 9mm out of the holster. Pulling back the slide, I jacked a round into the chamber. "Now you're locked and loaded."

Suzu put on her own belt and copied me getting the feel for the Earther weapon. Her wide grin reassured me that she was happy with what I had given her. She looked down at the belt and felt the pouches that lined each side and back. "What's in these?"

"Ammo for the pistol."

"Uhm, how long will it take us to get to this base?" She looked around at all the weapons and then back at me. "How much trouble are you expecting."

"Hopefully, it should only take us four days or so, but I figure it would be better to be loaded for trouble and not find any than to find it and have not enough weapons to deal with it."

Suzu smiled and nodded. "You, Tanya, would make a great Heoheska warrior."

"Thanks, I think. But now that we are armed I think we should get going, don't you?" Suzu took a deep breath and nodded as I moved to pack the last of our stuff.

The armored unit moved through the mountain pass with care. The two-lane road they were traveling on only allowed two of the heavy vehicles to move side by side. The lead truck unknowing tripped a thin wire, arming the weapons to either side of the road. Two more of the trucks passed. The tanks followed and were in the line of fire when the missiles flew from the tree line on each side.

The right-hand tank was lucky. It was riding the side of the road and the hillside which deflected the four missiles up and into the air before they could arm. They flew over the other tank and impacted on the left side of the road.

The left-hand tank was flat to the tree line and took all four missiles at the base of the turret. The first two missiles impacted the armor ripping the metal open. The second two hit the fuel lines that ran along the base of the turret.

There was a thundering noise and the turret flipped into the air followed by a fireball and dark smoke. The first tank sped past its dead companion while the turret came down on top of a fuel carrier, riding close behind the tank, turning it and the troop truck next to it into flaming death.

The rest of the unit sent tracer fire into each side of the woods until all the trees were cut down and small fires blazed on each side of the road. After a few minutes, the firing stopped and the remaining vehicles moved up the hill and around the burning ones. Moving, relentlessly, on to their destination.

Camouflaged eyes watched from above. After the Heoheska vehicles disappeared, they radioed in the results. Once done with that chore, the two soldiers carefully moved back to their own vehicle and raced north.

Chapter 15

Stopping, I held up a hand and looked back to the south. I could see a thin dark smoke trail rising into the air. Suzu slid up next to me and looked in the same direction. "Someone is having a very bad day," I whispered.

I saw her nod out the corner of my eye. "Probably an armored vehicle." More smoke rose in the air and we could hear just the faintest of sounds from that direction and the dark cloud grew. "More than one looks like."

Watching the smoke expand and trail off as the breeze took it further south, I had to agree with her. Those were probably Heoheska armored vehicles. The question was what took them out? Turning, I looked ahead for Bo Jangles and saw the tall grass barely moving about twenty feet in front of us. "Come on, we can't worry about whatever is happening behind us. We need to hit the store and pick up a few items before we head out again.

"Looking to run into more trouble with those orcs, Tanya?"

I patted the minigun that hung at my side and laughed. "If those guys bother us this time, I'll have a little surprise for them. Now let's get moving."

"Are you sure that you know where you're going, human?"

I pointed at the snow-covered mountaintop that looked down on the foothills in front of it. "That's Mount Baker, we can hardly miss it, can we?"

"Guess not. Lead on."

We started down the road when I looked around and realized I didn't see Bo anywhere. "Hey, Bo, you okay? Where are you?"

"I'm up at the crossroads here waiting for the two of you to finish with your break, girl." I laughed at the snarky tone of the cat ringing in my head as I saw her step out of the tall grass at the cross street before us. She shook herself and stretched under the pack she had strapped to her back. *"And, by the way, I'm a cat not a damn pack mule."*

Suzu laughed beside me as we got closer to Bo. "She doesn't look happy, your pet that is."

Bo sneered at the alien. *"Tell that overgrown kitty: brilliant observation. Did she figure that out all by herself or did she have help with it?"*

I laughed, shaking my head as we caught up with Bo. The alien glanced at me then glared down at the cat. "What did that overgrown fleabag say? Did she say something bad about me?"

I groaned. These two always going at each other might make the long hike even longer. I glanced down at Bo then looked at Suzu and grimaced at their sour faces. "Okay, you two need to make up and be friends or we won't get far. I'll need both of you helping if we're going to find this base."

The two of them glared at each other for a few more seconds then I saw the tension leave the alien's shoulders. "Alright. You're right. We need to help each other or die, I guess."

"I think I'd rather die, you . . ."

"BO!"

"Fine, fine, I'll be nice to the overgrown kitty. Alright?"

Suzu looked between the two of us and I laughed. "Bo said she would love to be friends too."

"That. Is. Not. What. I. Said. Girl."

"I doubt that is exactly what she said, but I'll take it."

Smiling, I nodded at my two friends. "Close enough. Now let's go shopping."

An hour later we were in the same small grove of trees we had been in the other day looking at the gaping doors of the old Wal-Mart. Dropping our packs behind some trees, we were once again waiting for Bo to make a quick check of the store's perimeter. Suzu shifted in the grass next to me and whispered, "You know the last time she did this she missed the other orcs in the store and we got in a whole lot of trouble."

I glared over at the alien. "Think you can do any better than she can?"

The alien sniffed the air and then shook her head. "I'm not sure what all the smells mean. But I'm sure if I did that I wouldn't have made that mistake."

I was going to answer when I heard the slightest movement in front of us. "Bo?"

"Hush, Tanya. We need to leave here now." Bo's voice rang in my head an anxious note tinting it as she stalked quietly out of the brush in front of us.

"What's the problem?" I whispered.

"Dogs! The worst of the worst mutants."

That's when the wind shifted and I caught the stink of a wild dog pack. That musky, wet smell that seemed to hang in the air wherever the mutants showed. "Damn."

Hearing a low growl next to me, I saw what little fur Suzu had was all ruffled up. Her face was scrunched up in a silent snarl. "What the hell is that smell?"

"It's a wild dog pack."

"Dogs? Oh. You mean the canine species that you humans tamed?"

"Yeah."

"You know this really is not the time to talk about sub-species of animals. We really need to leave here and go find another place to get your stuff."

I shook my head and looked at the store. Then at Suzu. "I'm going in. You two can stay here, but I want the gear in this store."

"You are just being stubborn, girl. We need to find your stuff somewhere else."

I glanced over at Bo then back to the alien. "You can stay here if you want. I'll be right back." Before I gave either of them a chance to say anything, I sprung up and started across the road for the doors. I shifted the minigun so that it pointed straight ahead, ready to take out anything that showed itself.

I flattened myself against the wall on one side of the doors and edged myself closer listening for any sound from inside. "Hey, wait." The whispered voice behind me made me jump about two feet into the air. As I spun around my finger, automatically, started to press down the trigger when I caught a glimpse of Bo and Suzu coming up behind me. "Damn, you about gave me a heart attack."

Suzu looked sheepish as I heard Bo's light laughter ring in my head. *"Sorry."*

"Fine, but you guys go back and wait for me. It won't take long to get what we need. I can get in there faster alone than with you two hanging around." Both stood there, silently, looking at me. Finally, I sighed and shook my head at them. "Fine. Then stay right here and watch the door for me."

I didn't wait for an answer. I spun around the corner and into the store. I ran at a crouch to the first set of cashier stations and kneeled behind them listening for any sound. Hearing nothing, I peeked over the edge of the counter and surveyed the area. Seeing and hearing nothing, I stood up and took a step away from the cashier station when I heard a snarl behind me.

Turning around slowly I saw three large dogs standing there snarling and growling as saliva dripped from their mouths. I could see that all three were mutants by their size. Plus, the mouth full of razor-sharp teeth which wouldn't let the canine mutant's mouths fully close was also a giveaway.

"Nice puppies? How about we all go over to the pet section and I open you some nice cans of Alpo?"

The three took a step forward moving as one unit when I caught their thoughts. Yeah, they had no intention of waiting for me to open pet food when they have a walking meat feast in front of them. I tried to raise the barrel of my minigun up when the mutants in front of me took another step forward, growling. There was no way I was going to get my weapon up before I became dog chow. I was so screwed.

Suzu looked over at the door and then down at Bo. "I don't know about you, but I have no intention of staying out here. The cat looked up at the alien and blinked as she nodded.

Both moved quietly through the doors when they heard Tanya's voice in front of them. Suzu and Bo passed the open doorway of a restaurant giving a quick peek inside when they heard the low growl in front of them. They quietly rushed over to the next wall and peeked around it seeing three massive dogs standing in front of Tanya.

Suzu took two steps away from the wall as she pointed the minigun she had toward the four bodies in front of her. She watched Tanya's eyes go wide as she yelled, "TANYA! JUMP!"

I watched the alien take a step from the wall pointing the minigun in my direction. For a second, I didn't know which would be worse: getting eaten by the dogs or cut in half by the alien.

When Suzu yelled, the three dogs were caught off guard and two started to turn toward the sound behind them. The third hesitated for a fraction of a second before jumping toward its next meal, but I was already flying through the air toward cover behind the cashier station.

When I hit the floor, I rolled as I heard the zipping sound of the minigun. Spinning and coming to my knees, I pressed and released the trigger as the third mutant landed behind me. The wall of lead from the minigun obliterated the front end of the monster into a bloody mist.

Taking a deep breath and waiting for another mutant to follow the first, I heard Suzu call to me. "Tanya, are you alright? I didn't hit you, did I?"

I laughed and stood looking at the two mutants that Suzu had taken care of. Her two targets were in the same tangled mess as mine along with the corner of the cashier station. "Nice shooting," I said as I watched Bo walk up to the two bodies and pee on what was left of them.

Suzu looked down and then at me. "What is she doing?"

I shrugged as I watched Bo walk over to the one I killed and repeat the process. "She's marking the kill so that everyone will think she killed them."

"Yeah, but you and I kil . . ."

"Not like anyone will think you two shorties are badass enough to take out these three. I might as well mark the kills since neither of you will."

"Does it really matter?"

Well, no, I guess not," Suzu whined looking highly disappointed as she watched Bo finish up with my kill and then walk up to me entwining herself in and out of my legs.

Reaching down, I scratched between Bo's ears smiling to myself. After a few seconds of this, I glanced up and looked around the store. "Bo, we're going to get our packs from outside so how about making a quick run around the store to make sure that we are alone."

"Okay, Tanya. I'll be done with a run by the time you two get back."

"Thanks, buddy," I said as the cat took off like her butt was on fire. "Okay, let's go get our stuff. We can gather all our supplies here and then spend the night."

"Yeah, but what about your father and his warning that we should get out of town today?"

I shrugged. "Remember that smoke this morning? I think someone is trying to slow down the warriors so we should have some time to prepare today and get going first thing in the morning. Besides, do you want to really spend the night out in the open?" Suzu didn't say anything but followed me out of the store to retrieve our packs.

The armored vehicles stopped at the edge of the smaller town. It had taken them most of the day to get this far. After the last ambush, the armored column had come upon a roadblock of massive rocks that blocked all lanes of the upper and lower roads.

The weary warriors had taken twice as long as it would normally take since they were as busy looking over their shoulders waiting for the next strike as they were working on clearing the obstruction in front of them.

After the roadblock, they had come upon the remains of the last armored camp of Heoheska warriors. All of the vehicles were open except one. Three warriors had died when they opened it to investigate and the creature inside leaped out tearing two of their throats out before any warrior could do a thing. The third died along with the undead creature when the lone tank sent a round into the vehicle.

Even though no more of the undead were found, the commander had the rest of the vehicles destroyed to eradicate any trace of the virus that seemed to be affecting his race. After that, it was a quick uneventful trip north. Once they reached the town that his map said was named Bellingham, the unit commander decided to stop and rest his tired crews before they tore this town apart looking for the humans who were causing so much trouble in this area.

Chapter 16

It took most of the day to sort through clothes, sleeping bags and other stuff that I thought was important to our little walkabout. Once we were done and no warriors had shown up, Suzu was in a better mood. Especially when I set up one of the gas grills in the back by the employee lunchroom door and heated enough water for a shower.

Hanging a camping shower from the ceiling, I poured hot water into it and we took turns getting clean. After scrubbing away the grime that had found spots on me I didn't know I could get dirt in, I felt so much better. Taking the last of the heated water, I cooked up our MREs so that we could have one good hot meal before we headed out into the wilderness tomorrow.

We were sitting by the back door of the break room enjoying the breeze that flowed in when Suzu looked up from her meal with a puzzled look. "Human, why did you not use this power of yours . . . I mean you know that fire thing when those mutants were attacking?"

"It's sort of hit and miss, Suzu." She stared at me trying to figure out what exactly I meant, I guess. I shrugged and explained as best as I could. "This power to produce fire and control it mostly happens when I'm mad. Any other time it comes or it doesn't. Understand?"

"Sure. I guess? Then why don't you work on this power and learn better control? It would seem to be the best weapon that you could have."

I laughed and shook my head as I threw the rest of my meal to Bo. "Believe me, before you came along I tried every waking moment morning, noon, and night trying to find a way to control this thing."

Watching Bo gulp down the rest of my MRE, I zoned out for a few minutes thinking of all the practice time I had put in trying to control my power when I saw the cat and alien stiffen and look toward the open door. "What is it?"

"Dog?"

"DOG!"

Scrambling up in a panic, I pushed the still hot grill out the door, burning my hand in the process, and slammed it shut as Bo's voice rang in my head. *"Chill, girl, they're still some ways away. I was only playing with you."*

Taking a deep breath, I looked at the two. "You know you could have told me that first instead of watching me make a fool out of myself and burning my hand."

Reaching down, ignoring the burn, I grabbed out a large red and white can. While popping off the cover, I stomped back to the door ignoring the sly smiles of my two friends. "What's that, Tanya?"

I tipped the can and started to pour the black powder in a large heaping line along the back door. Bo took a quick sniff, then sneezed and backed up laying her ears back on her head. *"You could have told me you were going to do that, girl, before you started pouring that crap around."*

Suzu watched Bo as she sneezed again then leaned forward and took a tiny sniff. I 'accidentally' knocked a fine cloud of the stuff in the air and smiled as the alien sneezed as she caught a nose full of pepper. Feeling like I had gotten a little revenge for my burnt hand, I finished laying the line of pepper and closed the container.

Suzu was sitting sneezing, rubbing her nose and watering eyes. Bo glared down at me from the top of the lockers, her eyes watering too. "That is black pepper. Any mutant dog that comes sniffing around the back door here will get a nose full of that instead of our scent. It also has the added bonus that this much pepper drives them crazy and makes mutants turn on each other."

"Yeah, and if you don't warn me next time, girl, I will show you just how crazy it makes me."

Looking up at Bo, my smile brightened as I whispered, "What's the matter, cat? Can't take it? You know I was just playing with you."

Bo huffed and went along the lockers far from the door and curled up in the corner. Suzu shook her head as she reached down into her pack and pulled out her med kit. "Since it looks like you two are done, come sit down here so that I can look at that burn on your hand."

I had forgotten about the burn until the alien reminded me. Then it came to the forefront as the pain reasserted itself. Nodding, I walked over to the sleeping bag where she was sitting and sat down next to her. "It's really not that bad. I . . ."

Suzu grabbed my hand and flipped it in hers looking down at the burn. "You're right it's not that bad, but it is starting to blister a little. This will help with the pain and keep it from getting infected," she said as she gently rubbed thick white glop on the burn.

Starting to protest, I slammed my mouth shut as the stuff suddenly cooled the burning and took away the pain. I looked down at my hand, held in the alien's warm embrace, and mumbled, "Thanks. That does feel better."

"No problem, I . . ." her voice trailed off as I felt her other hand travel up my arm and then land lightly on my check. Raising my head, I looked into those deep golden eyes as she leaned forward and I felt her lips softly press against mine.

I leaned into the kiss. I had been alone for so long. It had been ages since I had felt the warmth of another person as her arms moved around my neck, pulling my body into hers. I heard Bo's voice ring in my head breaking the spell of the moment. *"Oh, really. Some of us are trying to sleep here."*

Breaking the kiss and leaning away from Suzu, I glared up at Bo as I gasped from the feelings that were flowing through my body. "You are such a killjoy sometimes, cat. Did you know that?"

Suzu sighed next to me and I looked over at her giving her a shy smile as I got up from her sleeping bag. "I need to put some of this pepper over by the other door in case the mutants get inside the store again. I think it's going to get cold tonight so why don't you put the two sleeping bags together so we can share and keep warm." She nodded, a smile lighting up her face as I went over to the other door and poured another heaping line of black pepper along the floor.

After finishing that little chore, I walked back seeing that she had zipped our two bags together and pulled a couple of blankets in to keep us warm. Before crawling in with her, I turned off the lantern and then dived into the warm nest that she had set up for us. I rolled around some then Suzu's warm arms wrapped around me and pulled me close, her sweet lips seeking mine.

The hot white eyes stared down from the top of the old movie theater looking at the quiet camp before him. The warriors on guard duty walked in pairs around the camp with night vision gear, while the others were all in their armored vehicles buttoned down for the night. The unit commander was taking no chance of losing his whole command in a night raid.

But the creature that looked down on the armored vehicles was willing to trade any number of undead for the warriors below, for each dead warrior weakened the unit. He raised his head to the night and his whisper carried on the breeze. "Feed."

All around the armored unit zombies rose as one and fell upon the unit's unlucky warriors walking guard duty. First one then the rest got off one, maybe two shots before they went down under the crush of undead. Then the tide turned as flames shot out from the vehicles and roasted the bodies where they stood.

After a few minutes, the fire cleansed the area around the armored vehicles. The only sound was the crackling of burned flesh. The white-hot eyes looked down from his post a slight smile on his face waiting. Waiting for the commander to send out more troops for guard duty or cleanup.

The smile left his face as the armored unit started their engines and came out of their circle and started moving about two hundred meters down the road where they once again circled with all their weapons pointing outward. No more guards were posted outside the vehicles. This unit's commander was learning. Those fiery white eyes burned as they stared at the armored vehicles before they turned and disappeared into the dark.

Chapter 17

Rousing from the deep well of sleep, I could feel Suzu's warm breath on the back of my neck as her arm lay across my waist. I lay there for a second, eyes closed, just basking in the feeling. Enjoying the touch of another even if it was an alien. Then it clicked in. Something had dragged me from my sleep. I heard the sound of distant thunder while feeling a slight vibration through the ground. *"Tanya, get up. You two need to get up. I think the aliens are here."*

My eyes fluttered open seeing Bo's face about two inches away from my own. "Aliens here . . . what . . . Bo . . ." My voice tapered off to nothing as I heard more thunder and felt the shaking through the ground.

As my sleep-addled mind struggled to cope with thunder causing ground tremors Suzu sat up wild-eyed. "Oh damn, they're here."

I didn't see anyone but us three. Now, what was that damn cat playing at? "Who's here? It's just a storm, isn't it?"

Just then the thunder cracked louder and the vibrations grew stronger. Suzu scrambled out of the sleeping bag as I finally got it. The warriors had made it to Bellingham. I rolled out of the sleeping bag and started to gather our stuff together when I heard Bo's voice of reason cut through my panic. *"Whoa, whoa, girl. Chill down. From the sound and vibrations, I say they are still in the south part of town. Make sure you have everything."*

Bo was right. Us rushing around forgetting something important wouldn't help us in the long run. I stopped and took a deep breath as I reached over and turned on the lantern to see better. When the light clicked on, Suzu stopped and stared at it like a rabbit caught in headlights.

Seeing the same look of panic on her face that I knew was on mine, I took another deep breath to center myself. "Slow down, Suzu. Bo said we have a little time. So, let's make sure we get everything together before we go."

Suzu glanced at the cat and then back at me before she closed her eyes and took a deep breath as I had. She took another one as we heard more thunder and felt the ground shake under our feet. As dust trickled down over our heads, she opened her eyes and nodded. "The cat is right. They are close, but not so close that we need to rush."

A brief nod and I bent down to roll up our sleeping bags and blankets. Silently, Suzu worked on packing the rest of the stuff lying around our packs. We didn't rush, but we didn't exactly dilly-dally either. Within fifteen minutes we were loaded and armed once again. The only trouble came up when I strapped the ammo packs on Bo. *"This is not dignified for one of my status. Heaven help if one of my litter mates saw me being used like a common mule."*

"Oh, shut up, Bo. We all have to carry something. If you want me to carry the ammo then I'll just have to dump the cat food from my pack and let you fend for yourself."

Bo didn't say a word. She glared at me as she shook the packs side to side trying to adjust them then walked off in a huff. I chuckled a little as I walked over to Suzu and asked, "So, think we should go out the back door or through the store?"

She stood there considering the situation for a second when the thunder sounded again louder than before and more dust trickled on our heads. "There is tree cover outside the back door, right?"

"Well then, the back door it is," I said as I walked over to it and grabbed up a broom lying next to it. I swept the pepper I had lined along the bottom of the door to the side as best as I could.

Slowly opening the door, I peeked outside and winced at the sight. About twenty feet away lay three bodies – mutant dogs even bigger than the ones we had run into yesterday and torn all to pieces. I figured one or more of them must have gotten a good whiff of the pepper and gone crazy. I listened for a few minutes, but all I could hear was the clear sound of the alien weapons being discharged in the distance.

Stepping out the door, I scanned the area around us then looked back at the two waiting in the middle of the room. "It's all clear for now. Hold your breath as you cross the door so you don't breathe in any of the pepper I might have missed."

The two of them came out of the store eyeing the surrounding area as I had. Bo took one look at the three mutants and marched over to their dead bodies to mark them. "You know that is just disgusting, cat, don't you?" Suzu snarled.

"Yeah, well, you think that's disgusting just wait till you wake up one morning with a surprise in your boots."

I chuckled then shook my head at Suzu's puzzled look. "It's nothing. Just check your boots in the morning before you put them on."

Suzu gave me a sour look as Bo Jangles' grumpy voice rang in my head. *"Spoilsport."*

The sound that no longer could be mistaken for thunder sounded louder and the ground shook harder than before.

Now that we were out of the store, I could also smell smoke and saw a cloud of dust that was drifting up from the south. I started for the storefront when I heard Suzu whisper, "Where are you going, human."

I looked back and shrugged. "I want to see where they are before we head out."

'I don't think that is such a good idea, girl. We need to head east toward Baker now.'

"Let's just go, Tanya. We can see where the warriors are when we get further away."

Stopping at the edge of the store, I laughed. "Well, I'm glad you two are agreeing on something, but I think we need to see what they are doing, don't you?"

The two looked at each other. I almost laughed again not sure if the looks on their faces were because they didn't agree with me or that I had said that they had agreed with each other. After a few seconds, they both came stomping up to me neither one happy with the situation.

Fighting to keep my face neutral, I looked at the two before making sure that my minigun was ready for action. I peeked around the corner, gasped then pulled back. "What . . ." Suzu blurted out. Before I could answer, four mutant dogs ran past us and into the woods not even glancing our way. Across the parking lot, I watched a group of orcs slithering from one parked car to another before heading east as they kept glancing behind them.

"What's happening?" Suzu whispered as she moved up to my side just as a bulky mutant bear rumbled by us. I could hear the bear's high-pitched voice complaining in my head wishing that her mate was with her as she disappeared in the trees.

Glancing at Suzu then back at the creatures that were moving across the parking lot, I whispered back, "Guess all the damage the warriors are kicking up is driving everything east."

Hearing a snicker at my feet, I looked down and saw two cats a bit smaller than Bo Jangles standing and staring behind me. *"See, I told you I would be laughed at,"* my cat grumped.

"Shoo. Get out of here before I make you two into fur mittens," I said, half-heartedly aiming a kick in the general direction of the two. Their laughter echoed loud in my head as they bounded into the woods. I ignored the glare from the cat by my side.

"Poor thing, just ignore them," Suzu said watching the two cats disappear into the trees as she reached down and scratched between Bo's ears. I could hear the cat's purr working overtime as she took the consolation from the alien.

Watching the two for a second, I took another peek around the corner. "Oh damn."

They both glanced up at me. "What is it?"

"Come on, we have to move. These creatures aren't just running from those warriors."

"What?"

"Zombies. Undead. Come on, get up and move. We got zombies. The undead coming." Those words lit a fire under the two and before I could say anything else they were moving along with all the other creatures around us through the woods.

When I was younger, I had seen a movie where deer and wolves frantically scrambled through a forest fire together, neither group paying attention to the other. The only thought was to escape the sure death from the smoke and fire. I hadn't really thought that it was true until now.

Mutants, human and animal alike, moved through the trees away from the horde of undead that was shuffling behind them. Every once in a while, a creature would trip or go down hurt and you could tell when the zombies caught up to them by the short-lived screams that signaled the messy and violent end of their lives.

It seemed like we stumbled through the trees forever. The creatures around us thinned out as the undead took some from behind while the rest outraced us. Bo bounded through and over the trees and brush all the while yelling at us to keep moving.

We had made about five miles when we broke out into a clearing and there before us was a low white-painted building. Bending over trying to catch my breath, Suzu ran past me, stopped and then sprinted back to my side. "Come on, Tanya, we need to keep going."

Shaking my head, I tried to suck in air as I listened to the sounds of the zombies moving through the brush behind us. "You . . . go . . . on . . . I . . . can't . . . keep . . ."

Suzu grabbed my shoulders and shook me. "Oh, no, you don't, human. We are going to keep going. I'm not leaving you here."

My teeth rattled as she shook me and I pulled away from her my anger flaring. "I got along just fine before you came here, alien." I patted the minigun hanging at my side. "I'm tired of running."

"Did you see how many of them are after us? We would . . ." Suzu's eyes went wide as the first of the zombies broke through the trees, that weird low moan escaping their lips and echoing from the trees around us. Suzu grabbed my arm and started pulling me back toward that white building.

We backed up slowly when I heard the crackling of branches to my side. I watched as a small group of five zombies broke from the trees. Without thinking, I turned and swept my gun from one side to the other making that group disappear in a red mist from the waist up. "Well, that makes it easier to kill them," I laughed hysterically as I stared at the lower limbs that flopped around on the ground.

The zip of Suzu's weapon almost drowned out her voice. "Come on, human, move." I turned, taking my eyes off my kill seeing another group of half bodies lying about ten feet in front of us. Nodding, I backed up as I swiveled my head from side to side when I felt my back bump into the brick wall of the building.

"Get this pack off me so that I can fight, girl," Bo snarled as she knelt between us. Her eyes lit with a familiar fighting fire.

I bent down and loosened the strap of the pack as my eyes kept looking at the zombies that shuffled out of the trees. There were so many I couldn't count them and more were filtering out. "Where the hell did all these come from?"

No one answered me as I watched the undead slowly move closer to us. When they were close enough, I pressed the trigger down and swept my gun side to side watching as the fire that spit out of the barrels mowed down the zombies in front of us.

Seconds later my barrels spun empty. The fire that kept the zombies at bay dead like them. I hit the release, pulled the empty magazine from the gun, and reached down for a new one. As I clamped the new magazine in place, I caught Suzu following my steps.

Pressing the trigger, I swept the gun from side to side taking out the next set of zombies but knew this was a losing battle as this group was closer than the others had been. My barrels spun empty again when I heard Suzu yell. "THIS ISN'T GOING TO WORK!"

I was half turned, reaching down for a new magazine when I caught a glimpse of the alien's fist coming at my face. My head exploded and I started to black out when I felt myself picked up and thrown upwards.

I hit the edge of the building behind us and rolled two feet before my head cleared and, standing, I ran to the edge just as Bo and the ammo bags came flying up and hit me dead center in the chest knocking me backward on my butt.

Bo bounced off me, rolled to the side, and came to her feet, snarling. I threw the ammo pack to the side and jumped to my feet just as I heard Suzu scream. "SUZU!" I screamed back as I looked down at the horde of zombies gathered about the base of the wall.

Not one of them looked up from the grisly task before them and another scream from below echoed in my ears causing a red veil to wash over my eyes. My arms went wide as the last scream from my friend tore out my heart and then a wash of red flame flashed out of my body and swept across the clearing and the trees in front of me. Everything on the ground or in the trees was turned to ash instantly from the intensity of the heat. Anger, loss, and sorrow poured from me until I was spent and fell to my butt on the edge of the building.

I sat there, tears streaming from my eyes and dripping over the edge raining on the ash that was shifting in the breeze. I heard the quiet footfall of Bo's feet come up behind me and felt her presence as she sat down next to me looking over the side of the building. *"Tanya . . ."*

Not looking up from the ground below I whispered, "Don't. Don't say a word right now, please."

The two of us sat not speaking a word as we listened to the Heoheska destroy the southern part of Bellingham. As twilight crept in the sounds of destruction died down. I stood up and swiped at the trail of dried tears on my face. *"I'm sorry, Tanya. You know, about the alien. I . . ."*

I looked down at my friend. "I know you are, Bo Jangles. I know you are . . ." I stared off to the south seeing the few flames from the destruction licking the darkness that was gathering around the city. As the night breeze picked up, I thought I could hear a tiny voice faintly crying. I put it down to my own imagination when I looked down at Bo and she stood as though she hadn't heard anything.

"What are we going to do, Tanya? Are we heading to the mountains to find that base like your father said?" Bo asked as she glanced up at me.

I shook my head and laughed. "You know he isn't my daddy anymore, right, Bo?"

"Uh, Tanya, what are you thinking?"

I looked south as the last of the sun sunk below the horizon. "He is the reason that all these zombies were here. He and the Heoheska are the reason that Suzu died."

"Tanya, I . . ." I turned my head at her voice and glared down at her. *"Uh, yeah, never mind. Who do we take out first?"*

I nodded as I looked south again. "We take out whoever crosses our path, Bo. No matter who it is."

"Alright, girl. I'm with you even though I think this is a one-way mission."

"You know what, Bo Jangles? I just don't care if I make it through this or not. You can leave if you want."

"That's what I was afraid of." Her words sounded so quietly in my mind that I wasn't even sure they had been real. I chose to ignore her anyways as I gathered up the minigun and ammo packs lying around the roof of the building.

Chapter 18

The two of us moved through the night, back toward the store we had left this morning. Back to where I had been happy and in love. Back to where Suzu was alive. The back door to the employee break room was still open and I hesitated for just a second looking in at the dark opening. *"You know we can go in the other way, Tanya."* Bo's soothing voice rang in my mind as she rubbed in and out of my legs.

"No, that's fine, Bo Jangles. There has been so many dead that I can't afford to mourn them anymore. I can only avenge them now. Let's go get what we need."

We walked through the room and over to the inner door. I swept aside the line of pepper along that door with my foot and opened it, my minigun leading me out into the hallway. A small flashlight that I had carried in my pocket was taped to the top in front of the magazine.

The light caught the flash of mutant eyes before we heard the low growl from the four we had surprised. Without thinking, I pulled the trigger. The flash of tracer fire lit up the narrow hallway taking all four out.

Holding down the trigger, I heard someone screaming in rage and frustration until the barrels of the gun spun empty. *"Tanya. Tanya, stop. They're gone."* My raw throat told me that it had been me screaming as I released the trigger of the minigun and the barrels stopped spinning.

I flashed the tiny light mounted on my gun from side to side seeing nothing of the mutants except for the mess that painted the walls and floor of the hallway. Hitting the release, I changed magazines before looking down at Bo. "Sorry about that."

Bo stared at me for a few seconds before I heard her voice in my head. *"It's alright, girl, but you need to get yourself together if we are going to do this and live through it. And I, for one, would like to see the morning sunrise, even if you don't."*

"You're right, Bo, as usual. I told you before, I can do this on my own if you don't want to go with me. I know that right now my head isn't on right, but I can't help it."

I could hear her laughter tinkling in my head. *"Oh, no, you don't, girl. You aren't going off and having all the fun without me. Besides you've never been right in the head as you call it, not since you found me."*

More laughter rang in my head, even louder than before. "Yeah, thanks, Bo. Don't know what I would do without you. Now let's go get the stuff we need. Unless you have another inspiring pep talk you want to give."

We walked past the little bits of mutants plastered to the walls and out into the store. The first thing I had wanted to get was some new clothes. Between being thrown to the roof of the building and the fire that had burst from my body, the clothes I had on me were pretty much rags.

We walked over to the sporting goods section and found some decent camouflage clothes that would fit along with another smaller pack and sleeping bag. When I was done picking out this stuff, some more ammo for my pistol and some freeze-dried food that even the orcs wouldn't touch, I walked over to the front counter of the sporting goods center and looked down at the knives in the case.

"Uh, Tanya, just how close are you planning on getting to the aliens?"

Looking down, I smiled at her then broke the side of the glass case with the end of my minigun. I pulled out two long bowie knives and strapped one on each side of my belt, along with a smaller one behind my back. *"Okay, I take it you plan to get very, very close then."*

Shouldering my pack and adjusting my weapons, I gave one last look around the store then glanced down at Bo. "Let's go."

"Where are we going, Tanya?"

"Home."

"Home? You mean we're going home, home? But why are we going there, girl?" I didn't answer, I just walked out the door of the store and headed south toward my home. I figured Bo would find out soon enough why I wanted to go there.

Two hours later we were inside the house. I found some MREs and exchanged them for the freeze-dried stuff I had picked up from the store. I threw in a few cat treats that I knew Bo loved before I headed over to another trap door under a large dresser.

"Tanya, no. You know that you're not supposed to use any of that stuff. Your father said . . ." My head snapped up and around, glaring at the mention of my daddy. *"Okay then. Never mind, I didn't say a word, girl."*

I stared at her for a few more seconds until she wandered out of the room. I moved the dresser to the side and bent down yanking open the heavy door. I shone a light down inside the opening, grinning at the short boxes stacked in the space.

Reaching down and pulling out one of the boxes in the hole, I opened it hearing the pitter-patter of Bo's paws behind me. *"Oh, this will so not turn out for the good, girl."*

Pulling out the grenades from the box, I stuffed them in a cloth bag. I ignored the cat standing to the side and sniffing at the open hole. I closed the box and put it back when the bag was full. Pulling out another box, I watched Bo's eyes go wide and she ran from the room. *"Oh damn, damn, damn, girl. You are crazy."* I chuckled as I opened the box and carefully slid the explosives into another bag.

When that bag was full, I laid one of the explosives on the floor beside me and looked around the room one last time. "Bo, we're going," I said as I stood with the mine in my hand.

Bo came trotting around the corner as I turned a dial on top of the round metal disk. She stopped as she whispered, *"Tanya, did you just do what I think you did?"*

I laughed as I tossed the disk back down into the hole and started walking toward the door. "Sure did. We have thirty minutes to get as far from here as we can, I think."

"YOU THINK!?!" Bo spun and was out the door in a flash as I bent over laughing. Then I stopped and looked back at the hole and hurried after her. It had been quite a while since my daddy had taught me how to set the timers on those things, after all.

We were a mile away when the night behind us went up in flames. The sound of the explosion echoed in the dark. *"Well, I hope you feel better now."*

Turning, I watched the glow of the fire that ate its way through my old home. "I don't know about feeling better, but it's a start, Bo Jangles, it's a start." Turning back the way we were going I reset my mind to planning the rest of the night's activities.

Two hours later, I was looking down at the circle of armored Heoheska vehicles camped at the edge of downtown Bellingham. Or I guess I should say what had been parts of downtown Bellingham. Now they were parked on the flattened rubble of buildings. Rubble that had been blown up and crushed under their tracks. Sometimes crushed so finely that I could see dust devils dancing around them as the night breeze kicked up. To one side was the ocean, the other three sides were cleared fields of fire courtesy of their earlier destruction.

I jumped and hissed into the night as Bo's voice rang in my head. *"Tanya, is this really a good idea? Sorry. Sorry. Didn't mean to scare you."*

I would have believed the cat if I hadn't heard that tiny chuckle in my head. Glaring down at her, I bumped her with my leg as I whispered back, "You didn't scare me. I was just concentrating. There's a difference."

"Yeah, sure no problem."

I stiffened a little as I heard the tiniest of sounds behind me. Without acknowledging it, I glanced down at the cat and saw her ears laid back. "Listen, Bo, why don't you go down there and do a quick recon."

"Uh, Tanya, I . . ."

"Just do it, Bo Jangles. This is something that I need to do alone, for my own sanity."

Bo looked over her shoulder before she disappeared into the darkness. I watched for a few seconds looking down at the armored vehicles to see if I could see any sign of her. A hiss whispered from the dark behind my left shoulder, "You know I never did like that cat since the day we found her."

I hadn't jumped and I felt almost like a wave of pride wash over me from the shadow behind me. "She is the only thing that has kept me sane, Daddy."

"What are you doing here, Daughter?" I heard sniffling behind me. I could feel the anger in the hissing voice, "And with the explosives. I told you that you were never to . . ."

Whirling around I had one of the Bowie knives in my hand as I pointed it at the creature that once was my daddy and hissed back, "You have no right to ever tell me what to do. Do you hear me?"

The shadow stepped back, its eyes blazing pure white-hot rage for the tiniest of seconds then it cooled as I watched. The creature glanced around before focusing on me again. "Where is the alien that I gave you? She should know better."

Taking a deep breath kept me from lunging forward and jamming that knife between those hated white eyes. "Your zombies happened, Daddy. The ones that you brought here to kill the aliens and protect me. The ones that almost killed me and did kill Suzu. That's what happened to her, Daddy."

A deep hissing sigh came from the shadow. "That was not my intention, Daughter. I . . . I lost control of them . . . I'm sorry that you were almost hurt, but you did survive."

Tears ran down my face and I lowered my head so that my daddy could not see them. "I'm alive because Suzu gave her life for me."

"Yes, Daughter, but she was an alien so no big loss."

Standing there staring down at the ground, my hand tightened on the knife in my hand as I heard Bo Jangles' voice roaring in my head, *"TANYA! DON'T!"*

Ignoring the voice, I lunged forward. The knife made a swishing sound as it moved through the air. I felt the blade bury itself deep within the body before me and the release of foul air that came from the unseen mouth. "Tanya . . . I'm . . . your . . . father."

Grabbing the hilt with my other hand, I yanked up on the knife with all the hate I had buried within me and whispered back, "My father died a year ago. You. Are. Nothing. To. Me," I whispered twisting the knife first one way and then the other on each word.

Chapter 19

You would think that when you stab a human as I had done to the figure in front of me you would have blood, guts, and bodily fluids gushing from him. But when I pulled the knife up until it hit bone and stuck all that came out of the creature in front of me was a rotten, putrid smell of something long dead.

I watched as that white light died within those eyes and the shadow crumpled at my feet into a piled heap of dark clothes. *"Tanya, you killed your . . ."*

I glanced down at the cat that was supposed to be scouting the alien encampment for me and quietly laughed. "That wasn't him anymore, Bo. That wasn't my daddy anymore. Not for a long time, Bo Jangles. That was a monster that they created," I whispered as I pointed down the hill.

Bo took a step back and stared at me. Guess I couldn't blame her. Even to my ears, I sounded a little crazy. No, to be fair to her, I probably sounded a lot crazy. I wondered for a second if that was a good or bad thing when you could admit that you were losing your mind, but then the thought went away and I turned and looked down the hill. "I thought you said you were going down there and look over the encampment for me, Bo?"

"Girl, you didn't really think I was going to leave you here all by your lonesome, did you?"

"Thanks, Bo Jangles. You really are a true friend. I don't think I would have made it this long without you."

Yeah, yeah, whatever. Now are we going down there and kill some aliens or are we going to stay up here and have a cry fest?"

I couldn't help but laugh at the cat. "Oh, we are going down there and kill some aliens alright. We're going down there to kill every damn one of them."

"Good, then follow me."

"Hold on a second, Bo." The cat stopped and turned around huffing with impatience as I shrugged out of my pack and dug through it pulling out the two bags of explosives. The grenades I strapped along my belt so that I had about a dozen of them hanging around my waist. I did a quick count of vehicles and laid that many mines aside.

Bo gave me a quick once-over and shook her head. *"Do me a favor, Tanya."*

"Yeah? What?"

"Stay far enough behind me so that if one of those things go off you don't take me with you. Okay? Because if they do go boom there won't be enough of you to bury in a thimble."

"Sure, Bo. No problem. Okay now, I'm ready, let's go." I stood took a quick look behind me at the crumpled clothes lying on the ground then turned to follow the cat down the hill.

It took nearly an hour of moving in and around the buildings still standing until we got to the point where the warriors had stopped their destruction for the day. Peeking around the corner of the nearest building, I stared at the vehicles trying to see the best way to get close to them.

"Stay here, Tanya." Before I could answer the cat was gone.

I blinked and she had disappeared in the night. I knelt looking around the corner waiting when I saw a glint of metal moving around one of the vehicles. Then I saw three more around the armored vehicles moving from one side to the other.

As I watched I saw something else. All the armored vehicles had hatches open to let in fresh air. My eyes wandered back to the guards moving around and saw that they were moving slowly as though they were bored with the whole process. Guess they thought that since there were no zombies around they were safe and sound where they were. As soon as Bo Jangles got back I was going to show them how wrong they were.

I reached behind me for the hidden knife at my back when I heard a scraping sound. *"Chill, girl, it's only me."* I turned around and there was Bo, all smiles looking up at me.

"You know one of these days, cat . . ." I whispered as she stared back at me for a second then sat down and started to lick her paws as if she didn't have a care in the world. "Okay, so how did you get behind me, Bo?"

"There's a line of rubble from one of these buildings falling that will take us almost to the water's edge. It takes you, under cover, to about ten feet from the nearest vehicle."

"Then what?"

"Then, girl, you need to move very quietly and quickly to get to the vehicles."

"Okay, show me the way, Bo Jangles, and let's go rock these alien's world."

"Uh, Tanya, there might be a slight problem."

I sighed anxious to get on with the night's job but knew without Bo it would be hard to get close to the warriors. "Okay. What's the problem, cat?"

"Humans."

I sat waiting for a second, but she just went back to licking her paw without any other explanation. I hissed at her. "Bo! What about the humans?"

Bo looked up at me then out into the dark. *"Oh yeah. Sorry. There was human smell around in the air as though they are close by. I even smelled some in the rubble we're going to use."*

"How close is close, Bo? Are they going to take my kill?"

Bo moved across the space separating us and put her front paws up on to my knees getting her face only inches from mine. *"Tanya, you know that I love you, right?"*

"Yeah, Bo, I know that. What's the problem? A couple of months ago you would probably have charged in and took half of the warriors out before I could blink."

"I'm just afraid that you don't have your head screwed on right and aren't looking at the big picture."

"And that would be what, Bo?"

"That would be that if there are humans here let them take out these vehicles and you and I go find that base in the mountains."

"I think I can kill a few aliens without any help from other humans, Bo, don't you?"

A rough voice came from the corner of the building. "I don't think a little thing like you could kill one of the undead by yourself," I froze with my back to the voice as Bo melted into the dark. "Turn around slowly, human."

I guess if you're going to attack someone you shouldn't spend all night arguing about it with your cat. "Sure, no problem," I said as I reached down with one hand and palmed one of the grenades on the front of my belt. I flipped the spoon off the top with my thumb as I spun the rest of the way around and looked up at the two warriors standing in front of me.

The bigger warrior reached down to grab hold of me when I jammed the grenade in my hand into the front of his armor and pushed him backward. He stumbled back into the other warrior as I dived back around the corner of the building just as the explosive went off.

Well, I guess there was no sense in sneaking around anymore after that little exchange. I pulled myself up and spun around the corner, my minigun leading the way. I saw that the grenade had ripped the first warrior apart and wounded the second. As he writhed on the ground, a quick tap of the trigger of my minigun and that warrior stopped moving. Bo's voice shouted, *"TANYA! MORE INCOMING!"*

I looked up and saw a dozen warriors halfway across the space between me and the vehicles when there was a whooshing sound and two streaks of light hit the biggest of the armored vehicles.

The warriors in the group charging me stopped and turned as the vehicle went up in a ball of flame that lit up the darkness around us. That was a mistake on their part as I ran five feet forward and swept the minigun from one side to the other. Not much was left of them as I watched six more streaks of light fly from different directions impacting all but one of the vehicles.

The various explosions lit up the night and the concussion blew me over onto my butt. Hitting the magazine release, I slapped a loaded one in the weapon and stood just as the last vehicle came charging from out of the smoke and fire. Slamming my finger down on the trigger, I swept the gun across the front of the monster until the barrels spun on empty with no effect.

Just before the beast ran me over, I was hit from behind and rolled around the corner. Bo's voice screamed in my head, *"ARE YOU CRAZY, GIRL? YOU REALLY ARE TRYING TO GET YOURSELF KILLED!"* I didn't answer as I unslung the minigun, threw it to the side, and started pulling the pins on the grenades around my belt and throwing them at the armored vehicle.

All of them bounced off its armored hide and exploded around it. All that is but the last one that must have found one of the open hatches. I laughed wildly as the side of the vehicle bulged then flames erupted from the openings. The vehicle rolled forward a few more feet then came to a burning halt as secondary explosions lit off inside it.

Feeling something tug at my sleeve I glared down at Bo. *"Girl, we need to move it and fast"*

I shook my head at the cat trying to make sense of what she was telling me as I heard more voices coming from the smoke in front of me. Three Heoheska warriors all came charging out of the smoke that lay thickly over the rubble around us. Before I could register what was happening, there were three loud pops and the warriors went down one by one. Oh, yeah, it was definitely time to leave. "Let's go, Bo, we need to leave and fast."

"Uh, yeah, girl, I think I already said that."

"What? Okay. Whatever," I mumbled as I ran over to the weapon I had thrown aside. I grabbed it up, slung it across my shoulder and slapped in a new magazine. I glanced down at Bo and then around as I heard more pops and yells from the smoke around the vehicles. "Well, don't just stand there, cat, let's move."

Bo huffed at me and shook her head before she ran off into the night with me following close behind her. Behind us, I listened to the secondary explosions, and popping sounds coming from the smoke with some satisfaction.

Chapter 20

We trudged through the night until we finally made it back to that white building where I had lost Suzu just this morning. I climbed to the top of the building and sat there as I ate a lima bean and ham MRE and watched the fires from the Heoheska armored column light up the late-night sky. It seemed this day had come full circle. Sitting there I wondered if today had been a bad dream. Then I glanced down and saw all the burned-out grass and trees around the building. No, it had never been a dream. A nightmare maybe, but not a dream.

Bo sat next to me chowing down on the extra-large can of tuna that I had opened for her. It didn't smell quite right when I opened it, but she hadn't complained about it and had dived right into it with gusto.

My eyes started to droop a little as I finished the meal and I didn't quite catch what Bo said the first time. "What Bo? Sorry, guess I'm a little tired."

"I asked what are we going to do next, girl?"

"Well, first, I would say that one of us needs to get some sleep for a couple of hours and then the other of us after that."

"Fine. You sleep first and I'll wake you in two hours, but what do we do after that? And if you say eat I going to poop in your boots as

143

you sleep," Bo snapped at me as she licked the tuna off her whiskers.

I chuckled as I stretched and yawned watching the last of the fires die as the early morning birdsong filled the air with their music. I listened to their music for a few minutes and enjoyed the peaceful moment figuring it might be the last in a long time.

"Well, what are your plans, Tanya?"

I stretched out on the roof of the building making sure that I kept my boots on. I closed my eyes whispering so as not to disturb that sweet music filling the clearing, "After you're up, we'll go and find that base Daddy talked about."

"We going to find a safe place to hide, girl? Let others be in charge and take care of us?"

I chuckled lightly. "Oh, hell no, Bo. We're going to go and find that rich man's base and find out if they have enough weapons to wipe the aliens and zombies right out of our area."

"And if they decide they don't want to give us those weapons? If they even have them that is, then what?"

"I'm sorry, Bo Jangles, I never said I was going to ask nicely for the weapons."

"Yeah, that's what I thought you might say, girl. You think some little girl is going to walk into a base full of adults and take their weapons. Is that what you think, girl?"

I yawned some more and rolled on my back glancing up at the last of the stars before I closed my eyes again. "Let's worry about it when we get there, Bo Jangles. Okay?"

"Okay, Tanya."

Bo Jangles lay on the edge of the white building listening to the breathing of the young girl even out and soften in sleep. She watched as the last of the fires died down, the last signs of the havoc they had caused. She was worried about her friend. Tanya had taken so many chances in last night's firefight.

She laid her head on her paws staring off into the dark when her ears perked up at the soft crying sound that floated on the breeze. She stood looking east sniffing the air. She caught just the barest scent of zombies somewhere east of them too. Not close enough to be a danger then the sound died along with the cool night breeze.

Bo paced back and forth staring east, then stopped and lay back down next to the girl. *"Probably just ghosts, is all. Not like there isn't plenty of those around nowadays."*

Sitting at the edge of the building, I watched the sun move over the mountains. It was so peaceful in the clearing, well, except for the tiny trace of black smoke that trailed into the sky from the south, but other than that it was peaceful.

As the sun chased away the morning chill, I nudged Bo awake. "Come on, lazy. Time for us to get moving." Bo yawned and rolled over stretching as I heard a couple of tiny pops from her and a snort. "What's the matter? Getting old, cat?"

"Stuff it, girl."

I laughed as she rolled to her feet and pointily flexed her claws as she glared at me which only made me laugh some more. Shrugging into my pack, I looked around the clearing then down at the cat. "Are we clear to get down, Bo?"

She looked around as she walked along the edge of the building sniffing the air. *"Yeah, the clearing smells fine but I catch just the tiniest hint of zombies east of us."*

Turning, I lowered myself off the edge of the building until I hung a couple feet from the ground then released my hands. I flexed my knees as my feet hit the ground then turned searching the clearing for any danger. *"Watch out below,"* I heard Bo's voice laughing in my head as she flew past me and landed with a loud thump.

She skidded along the burnt dirt for a few feet before coming to a halt. "Real graceful there, Bo."

"Oh, you're just jealous because I always land on my feet," she said standing and shaking off the dirt she had collected in her 'graceful' jump.

"Yeah, you're just the full of grace, cat. Now if you're done goofing off how about we get moving?"

"We're not eating breakfast first?"

"Weren't you the one that threatened me if I mentioned food when we woke up, Bo?" I asked as I took off heading east.

"What's the matter? You lose your sense of humor, girl? I was only kidding."

"Chill, Bo. We'll eat in a few hours." I gave Bo a pointed glance. "Besides it isn't like one of us couldn't stand to skip a few meals." Bo just snorted at me and didn't say another word. I guess she thought she was punishing me or something. Little did she know how nice the silence was this morning.

We had been moving forward for about two hours Mount Baker looming in the distance and over the surrounding foothills when I saw we were coming up on another crossroads with buildings on each side. Bo stopped sniffing the air. I glanced around and then down at her. "What is it, Bo?"

"I smell zombies. Maybe three. Maybe four, and something else. Something like dirty underwear. Oh man, that stinks."

Glancing around, I cocked my head as I heard that low moan that the undead made coming from the right side of the small crossroad. Underneath it though I thought I heard a tiny little voice crying. I listened for a few minutes then started to the left. *"Uh, girl, where are you going?"*

Turning, I saw Bo standing where we had stopped and shook my head at her. "Whatever it is, Bo, is none of our business. We're going around this way."

"Tanya, can't you hear that small voice? It's crying. Someone is in trouble. You can't just walk off and leave them here like that, can you?"

"Watch me," I said as I turned and started walking across the intersection.

"Girl, if you do this you will never forgive yourself. You will be just like your father. A monster. Is that what you are? Is that who you want to be?"

I stopped, my shoulders hunched as though the cat had hit me with a sledgehammer. Without turning, I whispered, "Wasn't it you that told me not to save Suzu. That saving her would just lead to trouble. Well, you were right, Bo. I just can't go through that again. I can't."

I was wrong then, girl, as much as you're wrong now. Now, are you going to find out what is happening or do I go alone?"

Turning, I snarled as I stomped over to Bo and glared down at her. "Fine, we will go and find out who is in trouble. There are you satisfied?" Bo laughed and nodded as we turned right.

We worked our way around some houses until we could hear the moaning of the zombies around the corner of the last house. I got as close to the corner as I could and took a quick peek around it then ducked back so I wouldn't be seen. "I thought you said four or five of those things, Bo. Looks more like about twenty of them."

Bo peeked around the corner and ducked back as she chuckled, *"Hmmmm, guess my count was a little off."*

"I ought to throw you out there, cat, and let you fend for yourself, do you know that?"

Bo chuckled some more then peeked around again before ducking her head back around the corner. *"Well, since we're here no sense in wasting our time. Let's just take care of these suckers and save whoever is in there, girl."*

I listened for a few seconds but all I could hear was the moaning of the undead. "I don't think whoever is in there is alive. So, let's go around and head east," I said as I started to back up from the corner of the house.

Bo glanced at me then back at the corner of the building, then back at me. *"I'm doing this for your own good, Tanya,"* she said then disappeared around the corner of the house.

"BO!" I ran down the side of the house spun around the corner, my minigun pointing in front of me ready to see my friend being torn apart by the zombies. I skidded to a stop as I saw that damn cat sitting in the middle of the parking lot watching the zombies whose main interest was on the building in front of them.

Bo turned her head and blinked as she looked back at me. *Pretty single-minded, aren't they?"*

"Yeah, I guess whatever is in there is more interesting than some mangy cat."

"Or a mangy teen," she snorted back.

Watching the zombies, I could see that they were assembled around the front of the plate glass windows and doors of a small store. It was one of those places that these small towns had. They always seemed to carry a little of everything for their customers so that they didn't have to go too far to shop.

Slowly walking across the parking lot, I moved toward the end of the store. *"Uhm, girl, what are you doing?"*

Keeping my voice low, I shuffled closer to the building. "If I shoot now from where I was, Bo, I going to take out the windows and doors maybe killing whoever is in there."

I was even with the horde of undead along the front of the building when I glanced back at Bo to make sure she was out of range of my weapon when I heard the zombies moaning change. I looked back at them and saw that all their dead eyes were looking straight at me.

Oops, that's not good. I saw them turn as a group as I pressed the trigger of the minigun. The zipping sound from the gun was loud. I didn't even have to sweep it side to side as the undead shuffled straight toward me and into the hail of lead that tore them apart. "Damn!" I whispered as the barrels spun around on empty. The windows and doors and the sidewalk were covered from one side to the other with the remains of the undead or what was left of them.

As I changed the empty magazine out with my last loaded one, I walked down the sidewalk toward the glass doors of the store. I stopped and took a quick peek around before looking through the glass inside. *"Oh damn. That's gross."* I laughed as I looked down at Bo shaking gore off her paws as she stood next to me. *"Yeah, laugh it up, girl, but you're not the one that has to use her tongue to clean herself up."*

I cupped my hands and look into the darkened store then stood back and stared at the door for a few seconds. "This isn't getting us anywhere."

"Tanya, what are you going to . . ." Her voice trailed off as I reared back and kicked one of the glass doors in. The shattering of the glass echoed through the empty streets. Bo looked at the glass all over the floor then back up at me. *"Well, that made quite a mess. I'm supposed to get in there how?"*

Scooping the cat up in my arms, I huffed a little as I ducked through the broken door and into the store. Once we were clear of the glass, I tossed Bo down on the front counter. "Man, cat, you really need to lose a few pounds." Ignoring the dirty look she threw back at me, I glanced around before calling out. "Anyone here? Hello? I killed the zombies. It's safe to come out now."

I glanced around again then looked down at Bo and shrugged as a scream ripped the air inside the store and I was hit in the back taking me down onto my face.

Chapter 21

Rolling along the ground, it felt like I had a loud wildcat on my back. Small teeth clamped on my shoulder as I heard a muffled frustrated cry in my ears while Bo's laughing voice sang in my head. *"That a girl. You almost got it. Ooooh, ouch. That looked like it hurt. Did that hurt? Watch out for those little claws . . ."*

Finally, I got my arms around the squirming body attached to me and brought it around and slammed it to the ground. Grabbing one of my knives, I was just getting it ready to plunge it downward when I felt the tiny body below me go limp and Bo's scream echoed in my head. *"NO, TANYA! DON'T KILL IT! IT'S ONLY A CHILD!"*

My arm stopped of its own accord as my breath came in gasps. I looked down into the dirt-encrusted face below me. A pair of light blue eyes stared back at me. I glanced over at Bo. "Thanks for the help, cat."

"What are you crying about, girl? It's only a little kid. You took on an armored unit of Heoheska warriors, but you can't handle one little child? Some big bad warrior you are, girl."

I glared at Bo till I caught my breath then really looked at the tiny thing lying on the ground. She was half my size or less and along with those light blue eyes, she looked like she had blonde hair and light skin somewhere under all the dirt. That's when the smell assaulted my nose.

Bo stepped forward and sniffed the child taking a couple of quick steps backward as she wrinkled her nose. *"Yeah, this is the one that I smelled over the zombies, girl. No wonder they were all gathered around the door. That's one ripe meal . . . sorry . . . child there."*

I nodded as I took shallow breaths to combat the smell rising from the child. "Who are you? Where are your parents?" Not a sound came from that little mouth. Fine, I couldn't get her to talk, but I could do something about the smell. "Come here, Bo."

"Do I have to? It really does stink pretty bad."

"Get over here and make sure she doesn't move while I get something to clean her up with."

The cat shuffled over andlooked down at the child then up at me. *"And how am I to do that? I'm not touching that stinky little thing. Wait, it's a girl?"*

I looked at Bo and shook my head. "Yeah, she's a girl." Looking down at the child, I spoke as softly as I could. "Listen, if you move or try to run my cat here will eat you, got that?" The child didn't say a word. She just turned her head and looked off to the side ignoring me and the cat. I slowly got up. Keeping one eye on the child, I moved around the counter looking for what I needed.

"If you think I would even take a bite out of that you're crazy, girl."

"Shut up, Bo, I've seen you eat tuna that's sat out for a month so quit complaining and just watch her."

"Yeah, that tuna could've been sitting out for a year and it still would've smelled better than this thing."

Ten minutes later, I had two large wash buckets set up with bubbles floating at the top of each. A small pile rags and some towels were set next to them. Through it all, the child had just laid there quietly as she watched me set up the wash area. Walking over, I kneeled next to her. "Well, little one, it's bath time. Sorry the water is cold but if you're coming with us you need to be a lot cleaner than you are or you're going to attract every zombie for miles around."

The eyes looking up at me narrowed and the mouth opened. I swept the child up and turning, dumped her into the first large wash bucket. That's when the child started screaming and crying as I knelt next to it and started to strip her out of the rags she wore.

Bo was laughing as she watched me. That is until I threw one of the child's dirty socks her way, hitting her dead center in the face. *"HEY! You did that on purpose."*

I laughed back. "You think?" Once I got the child stripped out of the clothes she wore she suddenly stopped all the fussing and the cleaning went a lot quicker. By the time I was done the first bucket held water as black as night.

I picked the child up and dunked her into the second bucket seeing that I had gotten most of the dirt off her. I finished washing the rest of the dirt off and saw that she was blonde under all the dirt now floating in the two wash buckets. Pulling her out of the water, I wrapped the biggest towel around her and took the other one up and started to dry her head. "There now doesn't that feel better, little one?"

She stood there as I dried her off and Bo made another appearance. *"Well, at least she smells better now if nothing else, girl."*

The little girl looked over at Bo as though she had heard her and snarled at the cat. "I think she heard you, Bo."

"No way, Tanya, only you can hear me, right?"

The little girl looked at Bo then at me as I started drying the rest of her off and whispered, "You can hear cat?"

I laughed as I set her up on the counter and looked down at Bo. "Yeah, unfortunately, I can hear her. Can you hear everything she says too?" The girl didn't say a word but nodded as she looked between the two of us with wide eyes. "I'm going to find you some clean clothes so I need you to sit right here for a few minutes. Okay?"

"Cat not eat me?"

I shook my head and looked down at Bo. "No, she just looks like she will eat anything that sits still."

"You know, girl, you think you're funny but you're not." This brought a tiny giggle from the girl which startled both of us. Taking a chance, I looked at the girl and pointed down at the cat. "This is Bo and I'm Tanya. What's your name, little one?"

The little smile she wore disappeared for a second then she sighed and a ghost of it came back painting just the corners of her mouth. Her quiet little whisper sounded in the store, "Sonya."

"It's nice to meet you, Sonya. Now, I need you to sit right here so I can find you some clothes, okay?" The little girl sat for a second then glanced toward the store doors. I glanced that way then pointed at Bo. "The cat here will stay with you and watch to make sure none of the undead can get in. I promise I won't be long but just so you won't be scared, I'll let you hold my friend," I said as I reached down and pulled my doll out of the pack.

The girl's eyes lit as did her smile. She looked over at Bo who yawned showing off her mouth full of teeth. She scooted a little closer to me but nodded. I nodded back smiling at her then walked past the cat giving her a little bump as I went by and whispered, "Behave yourself and don't scare the child, Bo."

"Who me?"

Reaching down I picked up the rags Sonya had been wearing and tried to check the tags as I snarled at the cat, "Yeah, you, you fleabag." This brought another round of giggles from the little girl as she hugged my doll close to her chest. I tossed those rags aside since it was a hopeless cause trying to figure out any words on the shredded tags and decided I would just have to guess at the girl's size.

Two hours later, I had Sonya dressed and fed and found a small backpack that we packed with clothes and some treats that she liked. I got some extra blankets along with a hunting rifle and the ammo that went with it since I was down to the last magazine for my minigun. I had taken the time to sweep up the glass to the side of the door so that I didn't have to carry Bo out the door thinking we were finally ready to leave. Three bathroom breaks later we really were ready to go.

We stepped out the door of the store in the warm afternoon sun. I was halfway turned listening to the little girl who had found her voice when I saw Bo freeze in her tracks. I looked up from what Sonya had been saying when the snick of safeties sounded in the air. *"Damn. Sorry, Tanya, I didn't smell them."*

I looked at the four armored vehicles sitting off to the side of the store and the four camo-clad people standing just in front of us. Sonya had ducked behind my legs at seeing the people and I looked around before raising my hands in the air. "It's alright, Bo. My daddy told me about those uniforms they're wearing, they cover the scent of the wearer."

The four marched up to us and I was shocked when it hit me that . . . *"Tanya, they're all kids. What the hell?"* Bo's voice interrupted my thoughts as I looked around again. Sure enough, all the soldiers around us were kids ranging in age from probably eleven to the oldest being maybe my age or a little older.

The four stopped a few paces away when the oldest snapped to attention with the others and saluted. "Good afternoon, madam. I am Captain Bryce and these soldiers around me are under my command."

Glancing around, I thought maybe this was a joke or something and kept waiting for the adults to jump out of hiding. After a few seconds, I realized that they were serious and looked at the boy before me. "Well, uhm, nice to meet you. Uhm, Captain?"

A quick look of annoyance crossed his face then disappeared. "Yes, madam, Captain. My men and I are probably the last fighting forces in the world."

"Yeah, well, my name is not madam. I'm Tanya. This little one is Sonya, and that cat is Bo Jangles."

Bo's name brought a quick smile to the captain's face that went the way of the look of annoyance he wore a few seconds ago. "Alright, Tanya. It's nice to meet you. Now if you'll hand over your weapons to my men, we'll take you all back to the base for your protection."

I glanced around the group as the vehicles slowly moved forward noticing that the weapons on each vehicle were still pointing at us. I tried to give my best carefree smile to the captain. "That's okay. I think we can get along just fine on our own, thank you."

The captain looked back at me as his eyes narrowed. "Well, you see, Tanya, I wasn't asking you to come with us. I'm telling you that we are taking you in for your own protection."

I slowly moved my hand to swing my minigun when I heard Bo's voice. *"Tanya, that wouldn't be the smart thing to do. Think of the little one, girl."*

I sighed then unslung my weapons and handed them over to the two soldiers standing next to the captain. "Smart choice, Tanya. Now if you don't mind you and the little girl can hop in my vehicle for the trip back to the base."

I looked down at the cat and then up at the captain. "What about Bo? What about my cat?"

The captain glanced down at Bo then turning grabbed my arm while grabbing Sonya as he ordered the other two men, "Kill it." I spun away trying to get out of his grip and saw a flash of fur as Bo disappeared under one of the armored vehicles amid the clash of weapons. I screamed once more before I saw the quick flash of a rifle butt and then everything went black.

The portal outside Seattle was busy as the 4th Royal Guard Armored unit arrived on the planet Earth. These units were being sent to a planet that was thought by the high command to be dead. For a lifeless planet, it was taking a deadly toll on the Heoheska warriors already stationed there. The leaders of the Heoheska homeworld wanted to change that quickly at all costs.

Four hours later …

Bo Jangles crawled up through the darkness. As she fought her way through the black void, the pain from the gunshot that grazed her side, helped Bo focus. As consciousness returned, Bo remembered Tanya's scream. How the scream was cut short. How she had dived into the blackberries, crawling to the other side before the black overtook her.

"We should eat it now, brother."

"Careful, brother, I don't think it is quite dead yet."

"But it soon will be, brother. It soon will be and it has been so long since we've had something this fresh."

Bo listened to the voices and the flutter of wings at the edge of the bushes. Another wave of darkness roiled over her. Maybe the voices had a point, maybe she wasn't long for this world.

"See there, brother? Its tail twitched. It is not dead."

Bo heard the flutter of wings as air streaming over her kicked dust up by her face. *"No problem, brother. If it isn't dead now, it will be when I'm done with it."*

Bo felt something sharp peck at her wound and she hissed. Wings fluttered as the heavy body scrambled away. "Caw caw."

Laughter floated through the air. *"See, brother, I told you it wasn't dead yet. Now let us wait until it expires."*

"Great. Crows," Bo grumbled. Becoming bird food, not quite the way she thought she would leave this world. Fighting the darkness, Bo heard a tiny whisper in her head. "Kitty, help us. Help us, kitty. Please help …"

As the voice faded, it seemed to clear the dark void where she was trapped. It wasn't Tanya's voice, but it was a voice that needed help, needed her. Besides, the voice had said 'us.' So that probably meant Tanya was alive.

Another flutter of wings and Bo was brought back to more pressing matters. *"Come help me, brother. Come help me pull it out of the bushes so that we can enjoy a fresh meal."*

"Fine, brother."

Another set of wings fluttering closer brought a new determination – she was not going to become bird food. Ignoring the pain, Bo rolled into the body just as the first crow reached into the bushes to grab her.

Both bodies crashed out of the bushes. Cawing loudly, wings fluttering madly the other crow exploded off the ground before landing in a nearby tree. Bo landed on top of the first crow, snarling and spitting.

She gazed down at the crow underneath her and a smile played across her face and showing her wicked sharp teeth. *"So, now, who is going to eat who, bird?"* she snarled.

It was silent for a moment. *"No, please don't eat my brother. We meant you no harm,"* the crow in the tree begged.

Bo glanced up into the tree then back down at the bird under her. *"Funny. I could have sworn your brother here was planning on having me for a meal."*

Bo could see the bird's eyes go wide as it gulped loudly. *"It was a joke. Yes, that was it, cat, just a joke."*

"Yes, yes, my brother, the jokester," the crow in the tree laughed. His laughter died as Bo's eyes bore once more into his.

"Tell me why I shouldn't kill and eat your brother right here, right now?"

The bird under Bo gasped then struggled a little until the heavy cat put some more weight down on the bird's wings.

"No, no, wait. Don't hurt him. We promise. We will help you. Help you with whatever you need. Just don't hurt my brother."

Bo eased up on the wings. *"Fine, but I don't see how either of you could help me except by being a quick meal so I can get my strength back to find Tanya."*

"What's a 'Tanya?'" the bird in the tree asked.

"Tanya is the human girl who found me as a kitten. She is my friend. Other humans took her away."

It was quiet for a few seconds until the crow in the tree cawed. *"These others, they are the humans that live in the mountains?"*

"Yes, I think so. At least, that was where Tanya and I were headed. Why?"

"Let my brother up and we will help you. These humans are the ones that all but wiped out our family. My brother and I are the only ones that managed to escape."

Bo looked between the two crows for a few seconds before slowly easing her weight off the bird below her. The crow rolled to its feet. He shook his feathers out before flying up next to his brother.

"Thank you, creature, for my brother's life."

"Yes, well, my name is Bo and I remember you promised to help me find Tanya."

"Not to worry, Bo. We crows keep our word. My brother and I will help you. Besides, we have our own score to settle with these humans."

"Fine, so what do we do now?"

"Now, Bo, you will rest while my brother and I find your Tanya."

Bo was going to argue with that idea until a wave of dizziness washed over her. Bo sighed. *"Okay, I'll rest but just until you find where they have Tanya."*

Both crows cawed before flying off in different directions. Bo watched them disappear into the clouds before she stumbled over to a puddle and drank her fill.

With her body full of water, she squirmed her way back into the bushes to wait for the crows to return. As an hour dragged by, her eyes slowly closed and she was asleep.

About the Author

Robert is the author of multiple young adult and children's fantasy and sci-fi stories populated with strong female heroes and intriguing creatures pulled from his imagination. His characters are based on drawings and doodles that he has worked on since he could pick up a pencil.

Robert has traveled the world and met many interesting people. Now living in Bellingham, Washington with his wife and youngest child, he finds Bellingham and the surrounding areas rich with settings for his many novels. For more information on these enjoyable books please visit witchwaybooks.com and sign up for the monthly newsletter or stop by the Witch Way Books page on Facebook.

Made in the USA
Lexington, KY
04 November 2019